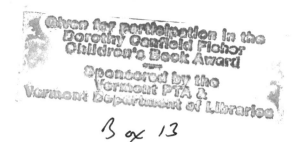

MEMORIES
Of
CLASON POINT

KELLY SONNENFELD

Memories of CLASON POINT

Dutton Books   New York

CIP Data is available.

Published in the United States by Dutton Children's Books,
a member of Penguin Putnam Inc.
375 Hudson Street, New York, New York 10014
Designed by Lilian Rosenstreich
Printed in USA
First Edition
ISBN 0-525-45961-8
1 3 5 7 9 10 8 6 4 2

To my husband, Sonny,
for his unfaltering faith in the manuscript
and to my mentor, writer Jose Yglesias

CONTENTS

MEMORIES
OF
CLASON POINT

FUNERALS

Prologue

$\mathcal{M}$y father was in his mid-seventies when he died in May 1965. He finally succumbed to the series of illnesses, operations, and lengthy hospital stays that plagued him for most of his life. Overcoming his doctor's dire warnings of little or no time left to him, his will to live was constantly fired by his desire to have just one more wish fulfilled. *If I can only last until my son comes home from the war . . . until I see my daughter married . . . until I hold my grandchildren . . . until my grandson's bar mitzvah . . .* he would think, always staying alive for the next important event until he could no longer fight off his latest illness.

At his funeral, I listened to the rabbi's narration of my father's life and the ritual Hebrew chants. My mind wandered to all the other times I sat in these same seats and listened to the same litany. How many times? I recounted them in my head: my mother, my grandmothers, aunts, uncles, and too many friends. Suddenly I felt tears on my cheeks, salt on my lips, and sensed a terrible empty feeling in my chest. I was not crying for my father, but for another memory of my father at this same place, a day some twenty years earlier.

On that long-past day, I received a call that Grandma Kellerman had passed away. I called my mother and my husband. But how could we reach my father and arrange to have him get to the funeral on time? We called the warden at Rikers Island and explained that since my father was quite ill, he would have to be informed of his mother's death gently. Could he possibly be released to come to the services at 11:00 A.M. the next day at Riverside Chapel? The warden said that he would try but would make no promises. My mother, angry and ashamed of her anger, begged us to "let Papa stay where he is and not be humiliated by his family." It was she who could not bear the humiliation of seeing my father this way. She could pretend, as she did daily, that he was a very sick man in a hospital, even though it was a prison hospital. If he did not attend his mother's funeral, she reasoned, wouldn't that be more proof of how ill he really was? Our arguments about Dad's right and his love of his mother won. My mother resigned herself to a terrible ordeal.

The morning of Grandma's funeral was a prematurely balmy day in May. We arrived at the chapel early, parked our car in the funeral cortege, and went for a cup of coffee in a small candy store next to the chapel. Again, I called Rikers Island. The warden said that all the arrangements had been made and my father and guards were on their way to the funeral services. Why did my elderly father, who weighed no more than a hundred pounds, need guards? Would they give him clothes appropriate for a funeral? I did not ask the warden these other questions. I asked my husband, and he reassured me with "They know what to do."

We had another cup of coffee to gird ourselves for whatever we would encounter inside Riverside Chapel. We waited on the corner, looking into every car that passed or parked nearby. My heart jumped when I saw the car, a nondescript gray sedan, ordinary looking except for the license plate. A man emerged from the front door. He held the back door open and my father came out, accompanied by a second man. My father was in handcuffs.

He looked old and frail in clothes much too large for him, borrowed for the occasion. I ran to him and we clung to each other, our tears running down our faces and into our necks, mingling as if they came from one person. The first guard whispered something to the other one. He removed the handcuffs. They let my husband and me walk into the family room with my dad, but the two of them were close behind us. My father placed a black yarmulke on his head. The two men did the same out of respect for my father and the occasion. When my mother saw my father, a deep cry rose from her throat even as she turned her back on him. My mother's constant fears that my father's illegal businesses would end in a jail sentence finally happened—albeit twenty years later.

My father's family was embarrassed: they lowered their eyes to avoid his. Only a niece and nephew said hello to him. The rabbi pinned a black ribbon to his lapel and cut it to symbolically show that Dad was in mourning. A disembodied voice said, "Will all but the mourners please step into the chapel."

The two officers tapped my father and asked him to sit with them at the rear of the chapel. We went with them. Then the rest of the family filed into the chapel and into the front row in single file—the mourner's walk. We all stood. My father's hand tightened around mine. I heard the rabbi's words as if I were not there. "Yisgadal, ve'yiskadash, sh'may rabo," I heard my father say along with the rabbi. This was Kaddish for his mother, one privilege nobody could deny him this day. As they finished, I realized that for me my grandma's funeral was the day that my father's entire family died.

The mourners filed out to the waiting cars. My father was walked to his waiting car—back to prison—with nobody except two gentle guards to hear his sobs and help him mourn for his mother on the hour-long trip back to Rikers Island. I clung to my father, pleading with the guards not to take him back just yet. They gently separated my father and me. He sat, head in his hands, in the rear seat. The man compassionately put a hand on his shoulder, and the car started off. I ran down the street, shouting, "Come back, don't take him away!

Please don't take him yet. Wait, please wait." The car turned the corner. It would be months before I saw my father again.

Someone took my hand and led me to the waiting cortege. I saw some of the family stare at me in silent sympathy. I hated them. It was not I who needed their sympathy. They were the losers, frightened people, who denied my father—their brother and uncle—a moment of love. I sat in the car, closed my eyes on the whole affair, and tried to remember other days with my father.

I was jolted out of the past when the services for my father ended with the rabbi reciting "The Lord is My Shepherd" as they wheeled my father's casket down the aisle to the street. We walked out of the chapel to the cars lined up behind the hearse. For a brief moment, I found myself looking down the street, half expecting to see the gray Department of Corrections car of my memory parked on the corner. Why couldn't I stop my tears? Memories floated to the surface of my mind. Another time, another place . . . a child crying as she watched another Corrections Department car drive away with her mother in the backseat . . . the rancid smell of vinegary mash rising from the still in our basement . . . my father taking me on walks along the Clason Point ferry slip as he told me stories of his childhood in the old country . . . the wonderful private house with my own bedroom, a painted sky on its ceiling . . . those days when we lived on Rosedale Avenue.

A memory of my maternal grandmother's words just before she died: My mother sobbing, inconsolable, at her mother's bedside . . . Grandma reaching out for my hand, holding it fast as she whispered, "Your mother knows why she is crying. When your mother dies, you're nobody's child." Memories . . . only memories now. As I write this, my father is dead, my mother is dead, and I, too, am nobody's child.

SOUNDVIEW TROLLEY

*B*efore there was a Triborough Bridge, a Whitestone Bridge, or even a Throgs Neck Bridge, there were two common ways to get to Long Island. One was the Fifty-ninth Street Bridge; it connected the borough of Manhattan with Long Island City in Queens. Or you could travel up to the northeast part of the Bronx, to Clason Point, and at the end of Soundview Avenue board a ferry to College Point in Queens.

The Soundview trolley ran from the Westchester Avenue subway station to the Clason Point ferry. At each end of its route, the motorman removed the coin box from the front of the car and placed it on a stand at the other end of the trolley, making ready for the drive in the opposite direction. Blue sparks flew when he disconnected the power arm to switch it to the wire hanging from what would become the front end of the car. I was fascinated by the miracle of a piece of wire making the trolley move. When all the necessary equipment changes were made, the motorman sat down on a small round wooden seat and signaled the conductor to open the folding front door, and passengers could get on for a five-cent fare or a trolley transfer ticket.

The conductor wore a coin changer on his belt. He knew the people who rode his trolley every day. He always had a greeting of some sort for each passenger as he collected the fare. "How's the kids?" "It's sure a hot day," or, acting as a messenger, "Saw Mike yesterday. He says he's okay, but to call him." He worried about everyone's health and safety. "Take your time. We'll wait," he'd call to anyone rushing to catch the trolley. He'd pretend not to see the boys who would leap on the back of the trolley to ride free from stop to stop. He was our friend.

The ride took us past woods, farmland, and some clearings. There was an area of vacant lots that contained an assortment of makeshift dwellings made from large packing cases and corrugated steel. Large oil drums were used for heat and cooking. Roofs were made of old rugs or shower curtains. The only people to be seen were men—old men, young men—all looking cold and tired. They huddled around the drums to keep warm and wore all of their clothes at once to protect whatever few possessions they still owned. My father would point out Shantytown as the trolley went by, commenting on how poor and alone the people there were.

"They've lost everything," he would say, "especially their pride." Then he would mumble something I didn't understand. "There but for the grace of God . . ." he'd say, and sigh.

It was very difficult for him to criticize his adopted country, but he did not spare President Hoover, who he blamed for the Depression. He told me that the men living like this in these desperate times called the areas "Hoovervilles."

One autumn afternoon, we decided to walk the mile or so along Soundview Avenue to our house. As we passed the shantytown area, an old man with a grizzled beard called out to us.

"Come here. I have something for the little girl," he said to my father. My father started to walk over to the old man, and I tried to pull him back.

"He won't hurt you. He just wants to say hello." He held my hand as we neared the man huddled by his oil-drum oven. When we were close, I noticed that it was only the beard that made the man look old. He was probably younger than my father. His clothes were worn thin at the elbows and knees, and the edges along the pockets and wrists were unraveled, giving him a dirty, unkempt appearance. He held out his hand and offered me a black-skinned baked potato.

I said, "No, thank you," and tried to hide myself in my father's coat. I felt a mixture of pity and revulsion and was aware, somehow, that my feelings were shameful. My father accepted the potato, rubbed off some of the black skin, and broke it open. He ate it with mock enthusiasm, telling the man how great it tasted, how it brought back memories of his youth, and how generous the man was. Then the man reached into his pocket and pulled out a wooden object. It was a figure of a deer whittled from a tree branch. He offered it to me, but I hid behind my father, again refusing his gift. My father told me to take it and tell the man how nice the figure was. I reluctantly did so, but when he tried to kiss my forehead, I pulled away in disgust. He did brush my head with his hand. I would not wait for my father. I ran off toward Soundview Avenue, my father close behind.

"Why did you make me take the deer? Why did you eat the potato?" I yelled.

My father caught up with me. He tried to take my hand. I pulled away in anger.

"You told me not to take anything from strangers. He was dirty. He even tried to kiss me, and you didn't care."

My father spoke very slowly. He was very angry with me. I had never seen him that way.

"I didn't know that my little girl could be so stupid and so mean," he said. "That man tried to give you what he probably wanted to give his own child. He lives here alone in this terrible place. Maybe he has a little girl somewhere he hasn't seen in a long time. He wanted to share his little food with us and to give you a little present. He wanted to feel like a person. How could you be so cruel?"

I began to cry. I cried because my father had scolded me, a very rare occurrence. I cried because I was stupid and cruel in his eyes. I cried for the man who was so far away from his family. I cried because I was afraid of the day when I would not have my father near me.

We never walked home again. I think the sight of Shantytown was as frightening to my father as it was to me. The horrible memory of it hung over both of us all through the bleak days that followed.

After it passed Shantytown, the trolley would continue to our destination. We lived in a community which was built in 1927 as a step up for the middle-class families who were living in the Bronx and Manhattan tenements. The trolley stopped on Soundview and Commonwealth Avenues in front of a group of stores. At one corner was a grocery store with a double display window piled high with rolls and bread. The store sold only one kind of bread—a seeded rye—and one kind of roll—a round, hard, crusted, poppy-seeded one. Any other kind of bread, rolls, muffins, or cake was home delivered by a Duggan's Bakery routeman who came to our neighborhood twice a week. Food was plentiful. Takers were few.

Large metal milk cans with large cup-sized dippers hanging on their sides stood close to the bread and rolls. You brought your own aluminum or white enamel quart or gallon milk container to the store, filled it with milk, and paid for the amount you took. You were trusted to be honest. If your family was more affluent, you had bottles of milk and cream delivered to your doorstep by Borden's Milk Company each morning. In cold weather, the milk froze and forced the cardboard cap to rise above the top of the bottle. My mother would skim the cream from the unhomogenized milk to whip it for a home-baked cake. If she was making a special treat for us, she shook the bottle to make a richer drink.

Sugar, coffee, rice, peas, beans, and other bulk products were stored in large red-lacquered tin bins with black and gold lettering to identify the merchandise. Scoops and brown paper bags were provided for the customer. After you took the amount you needed, you brought it to the owner of the store and he weighed it and marked the price on the bag.

Usually running a neighborhood store was a family effort, with husband, wife, and occasionally children waiting on customers. The whole family would live in the store in a little apartment behind a curtained wall.

My favorite section was the butter and cheese cases, not because of the products, but because of the containers that became available when the cheese or butter was sold out. The golden yellow butter was sold from a large half barrel. If you were the first to request it when it was emptied, you could take it home and make wonderful things with it. At home, we covered one with a soft pad for a footstool; another became a planter for a fir tree on our stoop. A cheese box, a foot long, three-inch wide, wooden rectangle, usually housing a loaf of cream cheese, was the prize most sought by both young and old customers. An entire family would fight over its possession. My mother used one for sprouting seeds, my father used one as a file box, and I coveted one for my teacher to use to make a flower box for the classroom windowsills. But my brother needed one most of all for his marbles. If you had a cheesebox and cut little doors in the base, you were the owner of the best immie game in town.

The butcher shop displayed its wares both inside and outside the store on large metal hooks. The sight of the whole dead animal hanging on a hook in front of the store window was disgusting to most children, but it was our butcher's advertising ploy.

The children's favorite store was Louie's, the local candy store. A candy store sold candy and ice cream cones, ice cream sandwiches, ice cream on a stick, school supplies, jacks, balls, and the boys' favorite: bubblegum with baseball players' pictures enclosed. A fast-trading business in baseball cards was a major spring pastime. Spauldines, rubber balls for gutter stickball, sold almost as fast as bubblegum.

A coin-operated wall telephone was at the rear. Louie used the kids as runners to call local people to the telephone. It was a service of the candy store, insuring Louie a small purchase in gratitude and the runner a small tip.

The best part of the store was a marble-topped counter that stretched almost its entire length. Louie made malteds and egg creams there. He knew every child by name. He made a dramatic production of preparing the malted or egg cream. "Listen, Sis, I'll give you the secret of a great malted," he would confide. "First, to get the milk ice cold." He dropped the ice cream from the scoop into a metal container an arm's length away, letting it go *plop*; then he would squirt the syrup in short spurts. Finally he winked as if letting us in on the real secret, took the milk out of a metal ice compartment under the counter, let us feel the icy bottle, and then poured it into the container. He turned on the switch on the malted machine. We would count to thirty, and he would then turn it off. One malted always filled two glasses, allowing two children to share it.

The counter also held large glass jars of penny candy, gum balls, all-day suckers, spearmints, dots of colored sugar on paper, wax whistles, a tin of sugar candy with a tiny metal spoon, licorice pipes and shoelaces, and green metallic-paper-covered chocolate peppermints. All sugar, but what treats!

If you stayed on the trolley past this group of stores, you passed more vacant lots and swampy vegetation. At Sound-view Avenue and Beach Street, a four-room wooden building was erected to house P.S. 69. Every morning we would line up outside the two-step covered entrances to each room. In the schoolyard we played "Actors and Actresses," guessing the stars who belonged to the initials called out by the leaders—our favorites were Charles Farrell and Janet Gaynor. The girls played catch or jacks, but the boys strayed farther to a nearby lot to play stickball or tackle, or even crossed the wide street to the swampy area to catch polliwogs and minnows.

In the winter, whoever was lucky enough to be named a plant or eraser monitor got to go inside the building when the teacher arrived. That meant getting warm sooner from the pot-bellied stove which heated the classroom while the rest of the children waited in the cold weather for the 9 A.M. bell to ring.

The early days of the Depression did not curtail any of our childhood activities. Whatever impact was felt in each household was never revealed by the children—like their parents, they kept family problems to themselves. Wisely, the principal of our elementary school dictated a dress code—a white middy blouse, red tie and navy-blue skirt for the girls; a white shirt, red tie and dark trousers for the boys. No child would feel deprived by not wearing the latest clothing fashion; we were all equal, at least in our uniform attire.

The week before the Thanksgiving holiday, each child was asked to contribute two cans of food for "less fortunate families." I cannot remember a single child who did not comply with this request; each child contributed to the pyramid of canned sardines and salmon, canned peas and carrots, string beans and corn, and the red-and-white-labeled Campbell's tomato and vegetable and pea soups at the rear of the classroom. At the time I surmised that none of my classmates were in the group of people who were less fortunate. How great a sacrifice this contribution really was for our parents was never mentioned. Family pride was at stake. The children were not to be shamed, and what little each family had was shared, if only to keep the family misfortune a secret, even from their own children, as long as they could keep up some pretense of survival.

The trolley finally arrived at Clason Point ferry, a favorite place for adults as well as children. In the marshes around the ferry slip we picked cattails; we called them punks and lit their bulbous ends in the belief that the smoke would ward off mosquitoes.

The ferry was a link to another world—Long Island— where, we believed, lots of rich people lived. For a nickel we could visit this place and get a glimpse of that other world. But Long Island Sound was more than that during Prohibition. It was a water route for illegal bootleggers. The rumrunners would transport the whiskey from hidden coves to secret boats and docks on both sides of Long Island Sound, the start of a long chain for distributing liquor. The network that started in Clason Point connected with buyers all over the rest of the country.

The trolley, having come to one end of its run at the ferry slip, now prepared for its journey back to the Westchester Avenue station, all for a five-cent fare.

CLASON POINT

$\mathcal{M}$y parents met and married through an arrangement made by a *shotchen*. Mrs. Klausen, the marriage broker, knew both families, knew that my mother's brother Sam was a successful songwriter, that my father's family was fairly well off. She also knew that my mother was nearly thirty and very hard of hearing, that my father was a *kranke*, a man in poor health. If my mother, the elder daughter, married, then her sister could think of marriage. The deal was made.

My mother was a romantic, a dreamer: she believed that stories with happy endings were possible. She had a Gibson girl figure, and her talented hands designed and put together hat samples. She had learned to read lips on her own, but still shied away from strangers, unable to comprehend them when they spoke, because she was unfamiliar with their speech pattern. Her married life was dedicated to her family; it centered around her home and children. She rarely left the house, except for a weekly visit to her mother.

She cared for my father and loved him in her manner, but she never understood him or his dreams. If hers were romantic dreams, his were dreams of success—the American dreams of making a financial killing, owning a house and land, and amassing a nest egg for security. To this end he invested in many get-rich-quick schemes and played the stock market.

My mother longed for a calm, quiet, even-keeled way of life, so her choice of a mate was not a wise one. She married a man who lived each day as a great gamble with very high highs and, unfortunately, the lowest of low times. Our home knew feast or famine, rarely anything in between.

My father's childhood experiences had colored his philosophy of life and living. He had spent part of almost every year of his life in hospitals. At the age of twelve, he had been pinned to the ground by a single-blade pitchfork thrown by a farmhand whom my father had taunted on my grandfather's farm in Hungary. The blade went through his body, tearing his stomach and part of his intestines.

After spending years in hospitals, undergoing extensive surgery, he was sent to a convalescent home in Switzerland. When he was somewhat recovered, he was sent to America with an elder sister and brother as forerunners for the rest of the family. A wave of anti-Semitism had come to their Hungarian village, a warning of things to come—land confiscation and the conscription of sons into the military.

My father arrived at Ellis Island when he was sixteen years old with a good European education, a suitcase containing a second suit, shirts, and a sweater, and a determination to prove the doctors wrong. They had told the family that his life expectancy was short, but my father believed that each day was a miracle and that the tomorrows, if he survived, would be even better. His jobs and way of life were always temporary, a self-test of his ability and endurance on his way up the success ladder in America. Every job was a new and different experience, each better, he hoped, than the last one. He was a trolley-car coin collector, a laundry worker, a paint salesman, a paint-store proprietor, a land surveyor, a building contractor, and a whiskey distiller and salesman. His dreams were big and always had the same goal—to own his own home and land.

After he and my mother were married and had my brother and me, he decided on a place for us to live. He became a real estate salesman for a newly developed area in the northeast part of the Bronx: Clason Point.

My mother worried about his new job, a gamble at the time. My mother worried about the end result of all my father's deals. My father would confide his dreams to me, most of the time saying, "Don't tell Mama. She'll worry. Let it be our secret." And my mother as frequently asked, "What did Daddy tell you?" So, at the tender age of six, I was my father's confidant and my mother's ears. In 1928, fulfilling his dream, my father moved my mother, my brother, and me to a small house on Rosedale Avenue in Clason Point.

Most of the inhabitants of the Clason Point section of the Bronx lived in an area two blocks long and three blocks deep. The houses were built with red brick, of no particular style of architecture, although they were supposed to resemble Tudor structures. Each block had a different style and a different plan. Commonwealth Avenue consisted of a row of two-family dwellings boasting a "finished" basement. Four-family houses were the feature of Noble Avenue, the rear entrances bordering on a farm. The street in the middle, Rosedale Avenue, had one-family houses—two-storied, semi-attached buildings with a driveway and two garages between each pair of houses. One side of the street had houses with an open brick porch; the other side had a many-paned, window-enclosed sun parlor. We moved to one of the latter during the summer of 1928.

The street was a mixture of native-born Americans and immigrants from Europe who had come to the United States after the Great War. There were Italian Catholics, and Jews from Russia, Poland, Austria, Hungary, and Germany who had settled first in lower Manhattan, on the Lower East Side or in Little Italy. Working eighteen hours a day, they saved their money earned as laborers—in sweatshops, on the docks, in stores, and as street peddlers with horse-drawn wagons—to achieve the American dream of owning their own home on a small piece of their own land. In 1928, Clason Point was the answer. You could buy a one-family house with a garage, a small garden in front, and a small plot of land in the rear. You could plant your rosebushes and hedges and

test your green thumb with vegetable seeds in the backyard.
And if you wanted to invest in income-producing property,
you purchased one of the multiple dwellings and became a
landlord.

My father bought a one-family house for us to live in and
a four-family house as an investment. After all, the rents
from the four apartments would bring in a good income,
leaving him time and money to speculate in the stock market
in 1928 and 1929.

Our street was predominantly Italian, with a sprinkling of
Jewish families. For no apparent reason, the Jewish families
bought houses on the side of the street that had the sun
parlors. The Italians seemed to prefer the open red-brick
porches.

The Esposito home sheltered a mother, father, two teen-
aged daughters, three younger boys, an aunt, two uncles, and
the maternal grandmother. The widowed grandmother wore
a long black dress and shawl—in the winter and summer—in
mourning for a husband who had died more than fifteen
years earlier. I can't remember seeing her in any color but
black. Filomena, the aunt, was a nurse. She wore a white uniform, white shoes, and a beautiful navy cape lined in bright
red wool, making her the envy of every little girl in the
neighborhood. She was the "doctor" on the street, telling the
mothers how to treat cramps, colds, and fevers, and bandag-
ing many sprained ankles and bruised knees. Filomena tried
to dispel the notion that garlic could prevent illness if worn
around the neck in a little cloth pouch. My family agreed

with Filomena about garlic, but swore by camphor balls or camphor bricks worn in a similar fashion. We were taken to a garage to inhale gas fumes to help our breathing when we had whooping cough. When Filomena laughed at these health measures, our parents humored her but still used their home remedies.

The two Esposito uncles were the celebrities of the street. They were musicians. Each day they would go to work wearing their tuxedos, ruffled shirts, black bow ties, and maroon satin cummerbunds, carrying their saxophone cases to the trolley. They played in Times Square with the famous Roxy Theater Orchestra, which gave performances daily between the many movie showings, and accompanied the vaudeville acts that followed the movie.

Mr. Esposito made sausages for a wholesale meat company. He often brought home strings of these sweet and hot pork sausages or large wheels of smelly cheeses, offering them to his neighbors. Since we kept a slight semblance of a kosher home, my mother politely refused the gifts, but my father would not turn down any invitation to the Esposito house to enjoy this food. Mrs. Esposito, like almost all of the mothers and grandmothers, stayed at home to clean and wash clothes, cook, bake, and listen to all the complaints of the many members of her family.

Having been used to small cramped quarters in their modest dwelling on a farm in southern Italy and even smaller quarters in a tenement on Mulberry Street in Little Italy, the

Espositos felt quite affluent living in a three-bedroom house on Rosedale Avenue.

Like the Espositos, the Ferraras had several generations living under one roof. Both sets of grandparents lived with them, in addition to their six daughters and their pride and joy, Joey, their only son. Joey went to City College as a pre-law student and worked on a freight elevator at night to contribute some money to the large household. The Ferraras had their own special dream. They were saving their money to return to a small town in southern Italy and buy land for a vineyard to produce the best grapes for the best wine ever made in their sun-filled homeland. While they waited to accumulate enough money to go home, they used their small backyard plot of land to grow grapes. In their basement they made wine, not as great as they knew their wine in Italy would be, but a good wine nevertheless. The sun, the rain, and the quality of the soil in their yard were not like that of Italy, but the results were not so bad for America.

Mr. Ferrara worked at a wholesale fruit and vegetable market at the east end of the Bronx. His day began at two in the morning when the retail greengrocers came to pick up the produce to stock their neighborhood stores. By midafternoon Mr. Ferrara was home again, and after a few hours of sleep he could be seen tying strings to his grapevines, planting vegetable seedlings, or pruning his rosebushes. The rosebushes were "for beauty," he said. With an Italian accent he quoted, "Man does not live by bread alone." The little garden was his passion, a symbol of his ownership of land. He knew that if he tended it and was good to the land, the land would be good to him.

Mrs. Ferrara felt the same way about her house. Despite the number of inhabitants, the house was always in order. Every surface shone with her constant polishing and that of the two elderly mothers as well. The floors were waxed to a high luster. "Cleanliness is next to godliness," she quoted, and she meant it.

Nevertheless, the house frightened me. The rooms were dark, the shades drawn to prevent the fabrics from fading. Evidence of their religion adorned every corner of the house: icons, crucifixes, reproductions of paintings of angels, sad-faced Jesuses, and Mary Magdalenes stared at me from the walls. The dark rooms were often illuminated by votive candles flickering in their red glasses, casting eerie shadows on the ceiling.

In contrast to the Ferrara house, our walls were adorned with reproductions of English and Dutch masters. Gainsborough's *Blue Boy* hung side by side with Reynolds's *Age of Innocence*. Rembrandt's *Night Watch* shared a wall with Vermeer's *Milkmaid*. Sheer curtains covered the windows, allowing filtered sunlight into the parlor, dining room, and kitchen—even if it did fade the fabrics.

I did not want to change places with the Ferraras' daughter Edith except on the occasion of her First Communion. Dressed in a white organdy dress, white shoes with a single strap, and white stockings, with a huge bouquet of flowers,

Edith went off to church. I had no idea what communion meant, but I did know it was a cause for family celebration.

One day our childish discussion of comparative religion resulted in an angry outburst from Edith.

Edith yelled, "You killed Christ!"

In tears I denied this. "I didn't have anything to do with it."

"I don't mean just you, but it is true. Jews killed Christ. And I should know. I go to church and I have to know the catechism before I can get communion. And it's true the Jews killed Jesus Christ."

"I don't know if that's true," I answered.

Edith said, "What do you know? You don't know anything about religion. You don't even go to your Jewish church."

I had no answer to that. As a Jew I had to bear the guilt with the rest of my tribe. I left Edith's house in tears.

Edith and I did not talk for weeks, until she decided that she wanted to be friends and was willing to rise above her beliefs by deciding to forgive me my sins, since I was not to blame for something that happened before I was born. Our friendship was never quite the same. I was once again her best friend, but I felt that she secretly wished I were not Jewish.

This was my first encounter with the feeling that being Jewish set me apart. When I told my father, he told me to reverse my thinking. "Why don't you tell yourself that Edith is the different one?" I tried out his logic, but being the only Jewish girl on Rosedale Avenue, dependent on the Italian-

Catholic girls for friendship, I decided I was different—at least, in that neighborhood. If there was any feeling to the contrary, it was never voiced.

The Amasanos had eleven children, five boys and six girls. They didn't worry about the boys' future but only about the problem of getting six daughters married—with a proper dowry for each. The girls had a similar dream, but they were not in such a hurry. Three of them spoke of going to high school and even college. Papa Amasano asked, "Why? What for? A husband needs a healthy wife to cook and clean and give him healthy fat *bambinos*—not a college wife." The girls sighed, but continued dreaming. Their father sighed and wondered if his girls were too American.

Their firstborn son, Paul, was studying for the priesthood. He was a wonderful young man who loved all the children on the street. When he came home to visit his family, he would organize baseball teams and tournaments. He helped build a clubhouse from old packing cases on a nearby vacant lot. He kept the teenage boys organized and busy. The girls were jealous of his attentions to the boys but admitted that Paul would look silly playing with dolls and jacks. When he was ordained a priest, the entire block participated in the party.

Crepe-paper streamers and balloons were strung from light pole to light pole. The street looked like a country fair. Long tables were heaped with all kinds of Jewish and Italian foods and drinks, contributed by several of the neighbors. Cheeses, salamis, pans of lasagna and Italian meatballs were spread out on one red-and-white-checked tablecloth that covered a wooden platform on horses; it stretched across the end of the block. Next to it, but leaving some space between them for the sake of the Jewish neighbors who did not eat *traif*, food forbidden in Jewish dietary law, tables were laden with fried chicken, bowls of chopped liver, and stuffed cabbage. Another table had sodas and lemonade in pitchers—and under the table was the local wine doled out to the adults, with adults watching the area for the appearance of the police. The last table was heaped with cookies and cakes made from prized family recipes.

One end of the street had a small platform for the band, a group of musicians brought by the Espositos from the Roxy to play for the festivities. An accordionist moved from group to group playing popular tunes and requests for Jewish or Italian songs from the old country.

Most of the neighbors got along very well, observing their own holidays, religion and cultural heritage, but enjoying the others' as well. The Jewish and Italian parents had much in common—love of their family, hospitality with abundant food as necessary ingredient, and the sound of constant yelling as a means of communication. The street was never still.

The only reserved people on the block were the Fairmont sisters, unmarried middle-aged schoolteachers. Since they were neither Italian nor Jewish, they were called "American Yankees" by the neighbors, who wondered why two women lived in a three-bedroom house "all alone." They were the only people who enclosed their property with a fence and high privet hedges, and who put up a flagpole out front. They

complained about noise, children, barking dogs, early morning milk deliveries, cars that backfired, roller skates, and
many other signs of life in the vicinity. They referred to their
neighbors as unwashed and illiterate peasants, even though
many of these immigrants had a European education and
background superior to theirs.

They called the police when two boys accidentally
knocked over the Fairmont garbage cans, colliding with them
as they tried to stop themselves as they skated by the house.
A policeman answered the urgent, hysterical call. As Edith
and I watched from across the street, the Fairmont sisters
identified the two ten-year-old, frightened culprits. The policeman tried to suppress his smile. He didn't see any criminal activity involved in the overturned garbage cans to
require his presence at the scene. However, he asked the
boys to pick up the garbage, put it back in the cans, put the
lids on the cans, and put them in their proper place; and they
apologized.

This did not please the agitated, angry women. "We want
them arrested or at least severely punished," they said.

The policeman answered, "It was only an accident. The
boys have apologized. They cleaned up the mess. What more
do you want?"

"Do your duty. You're a policeman. Punish them. I know
what I would do and I'm only a teacher. Uphold the law. Take
them to the police station. Punish them!" she said.

Politely, but with a firmer tone, the policeman answered,

"Ladies, I cannot do more than I've done with the boys. They seem like nice kids. They won't skate near your house again. Will you, boys?"

The boys shook their heads. Again they said, "We're sorry."

One Fairmont sister turned to the other and with a shrug she announced, in a voice loud enough for the entire block to hear, "What can you expect from the likes of children brought up by the likes of our common, uneducated slobs of neighbors. And what can you expect from a policeman who doesn't recognize riffraff when he sees it?" They walked into their house, slammed the door, and lowered the window shades to block out their unworthy neighbors.

The policeman sympathized with the boys and told them to avoid trouble by steering clear of the Fairmont house and the end of that street.

Mr. Greenspan, our next-door neighbor, was a traffic manager. We wondered what that was. He wore no uniform. We thought traffic management was what a policeman did to control the flow of the few cars in Clason Point. Mr. Greenspan used the sun parlor as his office and had an important piece of machinery on his desk—a telephone, also to be used in emergencies to relay important messages to his neighbors. The Greenspans had only one child, a twelve-year-old girl. The Italian neighbors could not understand why anyone would have only one child. Mrs. Ferrara remarked, "All those rooms and only one child?" She felt sorry for the Greenspans, whereas the Greenspans asked themselves, "Where do all those people sleep in just a three-bedroom house?" Both families managed to survive.

Mr. Wiener used his home for business. He turned his basement into a warehouse for supplies for his cut-rate drugstore. There were cartons of rouge, powder, lipstick, bandages, cold cream, and the like. We used to play store with the unpacked items. His son Danny gave me a jar of a miracle product guaranteed to make my freckles disappear. Like Filomena, Mr. Wiener gave medical advice to the mothers, limiting himself to prescribing aspirins or an alcohol rub or a mild cough medicine. He was referred to as "almost a doctor" and was respected by the community as an advisor and friend.

Mr. Wagner was a mystery. We knew that he had a wife, but we never saw her. He kept to himself and rarely even greeted his neighbors. We made up stories about him, about his past as a murderer or an executioner, or perhaps even a gangster. Mr. Wagner drove a hearse! He parked it in his driveway every night, and we speculated whether a dead body in a coffin lay inside the glass door. Each day he left his house dressed in his black suit, black hat, black shoes, white shirt, and black tie. His face had the blank expression that we believed was the proper look for an undertaker. As he drove past our houses on the street, we would chant, "The worms crawl in, the worms crawl out. They crawl in your ears and come out your mouth." He pretended he didn't hear us, or he shook his fist at us. We never went too far with Mr.

Wagner. We really were frightened by the man's appearance, which our childish imaginations made even more menacing.

The women worked all the time. After emptying the pan of water from the icebox, my mother would have a new block of ice delivered daily. She cooked the meals each day, since an icebox could not hold much food. Rugs were taken outside to be beaten clean. Clothes were hand washed, rubbed against a corrugated tin washboard and boiled in large galvanized steel tubs, then hung out to dry on a clothesline. Beds were made, floors were swept and washed, furniture was dusted and waxed—all that before a woman could take off a moment to listen to a radio story or read a book.

My mother was a reader, so we had many meals that were slightly burned while she was absorbed in some romantic novel. Before she married, my mother had been a milliner and designer, and she continued her work for the family or my dolls—the best-dressed dolls in the neighborhood.

The women had their roles to play—mama, wife, daughter, housekeeper, nurse, and confidant. These were a full-time job, from sunup to sunset. The women talked to each other about food and their children's health problems, but kept family troubles to themselves: "You don't air your problems on the clothesline." There were no outlets for their frustrations or fears. My mother quoted my grandmother: "Everyone has their own *pekel* [package of troubles]. If everyone put their problems on a clothesline, they would see all the troubles and they would take back their own." I always laughed at my grandmother's homespun philosophy, but the women seemed to agree with her words, and did what was expected of them. It was the only way.

The men went to work, brought home their wages, read their newspapers, listened to the radio, did yard work and a little gardening. They talked to each other about business ventures, the stock market, local politics, the state of the world, and their luck in having come so far since the old country. If asked what my father did, I replied that he was "in the stock market." I had no idea what that meant. My father read all the newspapers he could get his hands on, and the daily pile was stacked high with the *Times, Journal American* (with its Sunday comics), *Daily Mirror, Herald Tribune, News, World, Sun, Telegram,* and *Bronx Home News,* delivered by a boy on a paper route. My father said he needed the papers to check his investments and find out about new business ventures. With his own home, the rent from his four tenants, and the stock market, my father was content.

If home was a man's castle, the street was the children's domain. Snow, piled high, became the prize in the game of the King of the Hill. (The first boy who got to the top of the mound won.) But the first bud on a tree or a whiff of spring air really brought the gutter to life in a frenzy of activities. Sticks were cut off from old brooms to make new bats for stickball. High leather boots, with a pocket for a regulation Boy Scout pocketknife, were shed for new high-laced sneakers. A piece of clothesline was cut off for a new jump rope. Spring was here—could summer vacation be far behind?

We ate and drank and played in the streets. My mother had rules about eating food away from the kitchen table. We were only permitted to eat whole fruit on the street—or a slice of watermelon, "mickies" (potato cooked in charcoal), and, of course, ice cream pops or Eskimo pies sold from ice cream wagons on our street corner. Under protest, we were allowed to eat corn on the cob out of doors, since "all the other kids do."

Stickball was the street activity for the daytime, but the hours after dinner were reserved for Red Rover, War, Ring-a-levio, or Giant Step, played in the street by an unprescribed number of kids—the number determined by how many showed up each time. Even the girls were allowed in these games.

Spring was the signal too for carts to be built or renovated. To make a cart, my brother and his friends needed a pair of old ball-bearing skates, a plank of wood and a fruit crate. The skates were bolted to the plank of wood (like today's skateboard) and a wood crate was nailed to the front end of the board, with the open end facing the driver. Some boys added wood slats to the sides or the top of the box as a handle or stabilizer. With one foot on the pavement, the other on the board, the racers took off from the starting line to the last house on the block—the Fairmont sister's home.

The boys made guns from two pieces of wood one inch thick and five inches long nailed at right angles to each other. At the corner, a wedge was cut off. A rubber band was stretched from a nail at the end of the gun to the corner notch. When the rubber band was released by thumb, a piece of cardboard (the ammunition) put in a slot on top was catapulted a short distance. It stung the victim, but it never drew blood. My mother disapproved of all guns but allowed this one when my brother pleaded. "All the kids have one. I'm not asking for a BB gun." After the compromise, my brother got his gun, and I got black-and-blue marks all over my legs. When he finally allowed me to play any game using this gun he said, "Let's play Cowboys and Indians. You be the Indian." I was also the thief in Cops and Robbers.

Baseball cards were flipped, immies were knuckled in an attempt to amass more of the same. The cheese box owners started their marble game, winning even more of the beautiful glass balls when the marbles entered the slots cut in the box. The owner of a Boy Scout knife started a game of Territory by throwing his knife into the dirt in a prescribed circle, and thereby claiming his territory. There were boys' games; there were girls' games, the lines of division clearly made and adhered to.

Girls divided their time between the backyard and the sidewalk. Jump rope and double Dutch to the chant of nonsense rhymes, bouncing ball games to other words (like "One, two, three, alary . . ."), and jacks were played on the sidewalk. Stoopball was played against the steps, a ball hitting the point of the step and caught without a bounce adding points to one's score. A brisk trade in the *Bobbsey Twins* and the *Honey Bunch* book series occupied our mornings before outdoor activities began. Gradually the girls graduated to the *Nancy Drew* series or read serious books like Louisa May Alcott's *Little Women*.

Celluloid dolls were dressed in handmade clothes made from scraps of gingham or chintz left over from my mother's sewing projects. If I sat on a doll and pushed the celluloid in, a pin could be used to pull the damaged part back into shape. Spools became "horse-rein" projects. Wool was wound around four nails hammered into the top of the spool. With the use of a bent wire or hook, rows of wool were slipped over the nails over and over in a kind of knitting until a tubular braid appeared through the hole of the spool. The braid could become a rug or a small mat or a trivet when it was sewn in a circular shape, but I never saw a completed project. By the end of summer, the horse rein was abandoned. All games and projects had their seasons, and we didn't use a calendar to define them.

One long-term, nonseasonal activity was the making of a rubber-band ball. A small wad of paper started it, then it was covered by rubber bands stretched in varying directions, but always following the round contour of the ball. The object was to have the largest one ever—until the project was abandoned for a more exciting one.

We smoothed out peach pits by rubbing them against the rough concrete stoop steps. The object was to make a ring. Stoop sitting was a spring and summer ritual. There you heard heated discussions about baseball players and teams, the plots of movies related scene by scene, and confidences shared. Inane poems and nonsense rhymes were chanted over and over again. Occasionally, somebody would bring a song sheet with lyrics of popular songs, and an impromptu songfest would be held.

The only time the street was quiet was on Saturday or Sunday mornings. Taking enough food for a week's stay, we would attend the double feature, plus a cliff-hanger serial at the Ward movie house on Westchester Avenue. We would crack Indian nuts between our teeth and spit pollyseeds under our seats, to the dismay of adult patrons. We felt that they should have known better than to attend a movie at that time of day. The boys would sit up in the balcony so they could aim the nutshells and cherry pits at innocent victims in the orchestra section. If there was a special movie at the Loew's Boulevard, we made a whole day of it, seeing the movie twice and leaving a rug of shells, pits, gum wrappers, and brown paper bags.

Rosedale Avenue was an active, productive, and fairly secure street in Clason Point in the boom days of 1928 and 1929. Everyone had a part in its life and played his or her role in the expected manner.

Until October 29, 1929. The stock market crash that day plunged the country into the Great Depression. I didn't understand *why* it could happen but I gradually saw *what* happened in Clason Point. Our family and neighbors lost their jobs and looked for some way to clothe and feed their families—any way they could.

A. KELLERMAN
AND ASSOCIATES

The October 1929 stock market crash sent shock waves all over the world. The aftershock affected Clason Point for many years to come.

Each day, one could see some change in our immediate neighborhood. We noticed any number of men at home during the day. At first, they kept busy doing little repairs around the house. They painted the window trim, window boxes, picket fences, and any small area that could be painted in a day or so. They didn't undertake big jobs, because they expected to be back at work in a short time. As time went on they did the bigger jobs, cementing the stoop or the walk, painting the house or repairing a roof. Finally the repairs were all done. Now, the men came out of their houses and sat on the porch or leaned on the fence. First they read books, then newspapers, and eventually they just sat and stared into space—their empty eyes showing their utter despair. This inactivity was an alien way of life for these men; all their lives, they had spent sixteen hours a day, six days a week, working for wages to support their families.

The women no longer enjoyed swapping recipes. They couldn't afford most of the ingredients. Holiday meals, once a joy to smell and taste, were now a mock festivity with inexpensive and filling foods replacing the ham and the turkeys. The women did more work inside their homes and kept their worries to themselves. "Nobody has to know our problems," my mother said.

Shame became the common feeling of the day. Most of our neighbors said that they would rather starve than take the government's home relief, but eventually some of them accepted the food certificates "for the sake of the children." When Mrs. Wiedman put a nickel box of animal crackers on the counter as part of her food purchases with these certificates, an insensitive grocer said, "No crackers on home relief stamps, Missus." The embarrassed woman cringed and put the "illegal" crackers back on the shelf. If she was mortified, she managed to conceal her feelings better than her husband did. The Great Depression was aptly named. The men were crushed, depressed, hopeless, watching their families merely existing, sometimes with only the barest necessities.

Some of our neighbors still had jobs. The Esposito musicians still worked at the Roxy movie palace between the feature film showings. Filomena, the nurse, worked in a city hospital for less pay and longer hours, and was happy to be earning a salary. The policemen and firemen were still on the job. Joey Ferrara quit school to work at his freight elevator operator job full-time, feeling lucky to be able to bring a few dollars home to a family of six young sisters, a mother and father. And the Fairmont sisters, who still taught school, had even less respect for their inferior neighbors and were as contemptuous as ever.

By this time my father had decided that a bad law was meant to be broken. If he needed any justification, all he had to do was see my mother lining the torn soles of my shoes with folded newspaper or cardboard, or hear me say that I was hungry. He was a proud man; charity was not for him. He left the house each morning and came home each night with some kind of food for us to eat—apples, potatoes, turnips, or stale bread. Where he went or how he got the food was never found out.

My mother urged him to force his tenants in the four-family house to pay some of their back rent. He would answer, "How can you get blood from a stone? If you're so smart, you try!"

My mother went to the apartments to plead with the tenants for some money, any money. She came away even more depressed. She told my father, "They're even worse off than we are." With no income from the apartments, my father stopped paying the bank the monthly mortgage money and the house was foreclosed. Eventually, the tenants were evicted by the bank, and they actually blamed my father for not keeping up with the mortgage payments.

For a time, the local merchants granted credit. Ashamed to face the shopkeepers, parents would send their children to get food "on trust." I would ask, "Can I have a quart of milk and a loaf of rye bread on trust, Sammy?"

Mr. Freedman, the butcher, would say, "Okay, kiddie, tell Mama I'm writing it down on the ice."

I could not understand why he said such a silly thing. He was a kind, sensitive man who could not stand the sight of embarrassment or shame on a person's face. When you purchased a pound of ground meat, you got more than a pound with the ends and scraps added. He threw in marrowbones and knucklebones for soup. From the pound of meat plus eggs, stale bread, a little tomato sauce, onions, and spices, my mother was able to make a meat loaf for several meals. The bones and soup greens boiled and then simmered in a huge stockpot all through the days of the Depression. Soup with barley, split peas, or rice, added to inexpensively obtained farm vegetables and some bread, was a staple that could fill you up and stick to your ribs. My mother, a firm believer in the power of vegetables, was able to force spinach into our diet by mixing it with mashed potatoes. She also introduced kohlrabi and turnips, which were hers for the asking from a nearby farm. My father ate both of them cold, thinly sliced. The rest of us, unwillingly, ate them disguised in stews or, again, mashed with potatoes. A pot of soup sat on our stove over a low flame throughout those hungry days of my childhood.

The kitchen, a bright room with many windows and doors, was the hub of our house. French doors connected the kitchen and the dining room; another kitchen door led to a small breakfast room, and still another allowed passage through the pantry to the back door and yard. Glass-doored cabinets lined the upper walls, wooden cabinets the lower. Everything in the kitchen was white—white enamel paint above the white tile walls, white paint on all the cupboards, closets and doors, white sheer curtains on all the windows and the glass-paned French doors. The only colors you could see were on the patterned dishes and bowls in the overhead cabinets.

It was no wonder that the second most used part of the kitchen, after the white enamel stove, was the huge porcelain sink. If my mother was not at the stove cooking our meals, she was at the sink washing clothes and the numerous pairs of white translucent curtains.

An oak icebox occupied most of the pantry. The two-door oak chest held a block of ice in the upper compartment, necessitating frequent deliveries from the iceman. The lower shelves housed the perishables: milk, butter, cheese, and the ever-present blue glass bottle of seltzer. When times were good, the cabinet shelves were filled with boxes of cereals, bags of vegetables, and canisters of flour, sugar, and the like.

Every day began and ended in the kitchen. Reprimands, praise, sorrows and joys, past and future events, messages, stories, and serious conversations all took place around the maple kitchen table.

So it was in the kitchen one morning that I heard an argument between my parents. I was sitting on the steps leading to the kitchen and heard my father shouting. It frightened me. My father rarely raised his voice. His solution to most disagreements was to withdraw, leave the house for a while, giving my mother time to rage, calm down, and forget the whole thing. This time he didn't go away.

My mother yelled, "Are you crazy? We don't have enough trouble now? You want the cops to catch you? You want to spend the rest of your life in jail? You'll die there!" The words tumbled out of her mouth. The ranting was unstoppable. "It's against the law."

My father shouted, "Stop already! Enough! All right, so what do you want from me? Do you want to go on home re-lief? You want the city to give us charity? You want to make me a *schnorrer*, with my hand out? I'd rather sell apples on a street corner." Now my father could not stop the rage and frustration building inside of him. When my mother tried to interrupt he put his hand over her mouth and continued his tirade.

"You want to ask your rich brother for help? He's a rich man. He gambles away more money at the racetrack in one week than we could use in a year. I can just hear him and your other brothers. 'Birdie, we told you not to marry the bum. You made your bed sooo . . . blah, blah, blah.' Do you really want to hear all that?"

My mother looked pained. "No. But I still don't want a still in the basement of our home. What are you thinking?

Can't you ask *your* brothers for money? They owe you. They cheated you out of your part of the family business. They stole your inheritance."

Furiously my father yelled, "Don't bring my family into this! They didn't cheat me. I got out of the paint business myself. I hated it. Anyhow my brothers can hardly keep a roof over their own heads or feed their families."

My mother answered sarcastically, "But at least they *can* feed their own families!"

"I won't ask my brothers. They would love it if I came crawling for help. They would throw up to me all the mistakes I ever made. I'll never give them the satisfaction."

The voices grew louder and louder and louder as I listened. I put my hands over my ears but could not drown out the agitated voices.

My father continued, "I could feed my family if only you didn't close your mind to my idea. The still could make enough money to take care of us. Anyway, whatever you say I'm going to do it! Take it or leave it! I can't wait for a miracle to pay the bills."

"What do you know about whiskey? Who's going to help you? Who's going to set up the still? Nobody is crazy enough to lend you money. You're a nobody!" she cried.

"There are people. There are people looking for a nobody like me," he answered.

"Why?" my mother asked, frowning with the thoughts forming in her head.

"Because they need *me*. They need the liquor. I can make

it where the cops wouldn't think of looking for a still. Who would think of looking for a still in a basement in Clason Point, run by a middle-aged Jewish man who has a wife and two kids?" my father said, drawing the picture for my mother.

"Why don't you say it? You'll be a bootlegger like the gangsters who need you. You'll be working with crooks, lowlifes, bums. No, no, no, I won't have those murdering *gonifs* in my house! No, no, no!" she shouted.

"Calm down! You'll have a stroke. They won't ever come here. They'll supply the stuff. I'll make the whiskey. I'll package it. I'll deliver it to them and get my money. Stop worrying. All you do is worry. It will all be all right. You'll see," he said in a comforting tone.

My mother wouldn't accept his reasoning. "I'll see, I'll see. I'll see you behind bars and me and the kids out on the street. They'll make trouble for us. You'll see!"

"Enough already. I'm going to do it. I already said yes. I'm not involved with crooks. It's just a business. All I have to do is make the whiskey. That's all. So it's finished. Discussion closed!" he said as he slammed his hand down on the kitchen table.

My father noticed me on the staircase. He pointed to me.

"Sssh," my mother said. "You'll scare her. She doesn't have to know—she doesn't have to worry."

My mother was unaware that my father had already asked me about this idea of making whiskey in our basement before he discussed it with her. Once again, he had said, "Don't tell Mama. I'll tell her when I'm sure about it. Don't worry her yet. You'll keep the secret?"

The family conversation ended. My mother thought she was protecting me from worry. My father was just glad the discussion was over. Mother busied herself making oatmeal, coffee, and toast for breakfast.

My brother bounded down the back stairs two at a time. He said hi as he headed for the back door.

My mother called, "No breakfast?"

Mac answered, "Not now. I'm busy. I don't have time."

Mother asked, "Where's the fire? Where are you going in a hurry?"

"Out!" he replied.

"Out, where?" she asked.

"Just out," Mac yelled, his usual answer to this question. He left, slamming the back door behind him. Mac had no idea of where he was going. His destination depended on his friends and what equipment they had with them—bat, ball, glove. My brother's departures may have been vague but his arrivals were never secretive. The woosh, woosh sound of his corduroy knickers announced his presence.

Why did my mother continue to get agitated by Mac's behavior? She never gave up. She shook her head and asked no one in particular, "Where is out? What kind of answer is out? He's going to get into trouble. Out, out..."

My father left. I was the only one around. Mother had to reach out to someone. I was the only one left to talk to, so I became her confidant as well. I listened to her fears and her

worries about when all this would end. "Your father..."
she mumbled and did not complete the thought. "Your
brother ... they will be the death of me. What will become of
them?"

I was not supposed to answer. She was thinking aloud.
She had only questions for me. Questions with no answers.

My grandma's friends often referred to me as the *alte
Kopf*—old head—too old for my age. When my parents involved me in their thoughts and deeds I thought about which
was right. I didn't have an *alte Kopf*—I just worried as if I
had one. I was growing up.

The next day my father made arrangements to go into a
new business at home by setting up a still in our basement to
make whiskey. Rationalizing, he decided that he was merely
carrying on a family tradition of whiskey manufacturing that
was started in Hungary by his grandfather. "A. Kellerman and
Son, Distillers Since 1813," was launched in our basement
on Rosedale Avenue, on a direct route to the Clason Point
ferry and the illegal rumrunner who defied the Volstead Act
prohibiting the sale, manufacturing, or consumption of alcoholic beverages.

This started a new stream of people in and out of our
house, and it lasted for some time. Most were sporadic visitors; others became permanent members of our household.

My favorite was Bill, a Depression drifter who wandered
from town to town to find food and lodging and a "few pennies to jingle in his pocket." He drifted into our neighborhood and met my father at a newsstand. The two men struck

up a friendship, and my father brought him home. Bill became my father's "chauffeur," chemist, salesman, and friend. Even my mother liked Bill, because he was able to change electric iron cords, fix locks, glue chairs, rake leaves, and do all the odd jobs that my father's "all thumbs" didn't do. In exchange for a bed in the basement, a hot plate to cook on, and a portion of our family's meals, Bill was our jack-of-all-trades and the first member of our extended family. We never knew where he had come from or any other details of his life, but it didn't matter to any of us. We loved him and his happy disposition, his corny jokes and his constant singing.

Nick was another one who visited our house every evening. I had no idea what he did or why he was there. He had a regular part-time job at the Ward Theatre, a movie house on Westchester Avenue. He was the night watchman and janitor, sweeping up the Indian nut and pollyseed shells, cherry pits, candy wrappers, and other debris left by children who sat and ate through the double features and serials each week. While Bill was a handsome young man, Nick was the ugliest and most deformed man I had ever seen. He walked with a limp because of his peg leg. He had a huge wart near his broken nose. He was missing several front teeth, and he had a raspy voice that sounded as if he were being strangled. He had been a prizefighter before the war, and enlisted to go to France with the American expeditionary forces "to make the world safe for democracy." He lost a leg in "no-man's-land," and his voice when he was gassed by the Germans. He never talked about his war experiences. When I became used to his grotesque appearance, I was less frightened by him. I then romanticized him as a brave soldier. I had seen *All Quiet on the Western Front* at the Ward movie house and loved Lew Ayres as the German soldier disillusioned by war and its utter futility. I asked Nick what he thought of war, of being a soldier, and if he was brave. His only answer was brief—"I was just a soldier," he mumbled.

Nick was also a jack-of-all-trades. There was nothing mechanical that he could not do, from carpentry to plumbing, from installing a lock to breaking a lock, from digging ditches to gardening. He even did some sewing on a sewing machine operated by a foot treadle. He also knew how to construct a still to make bootleg whiskey.

If Nick knew how to construct a still, Eddie, another new visitor, knew the sources of supply. He had worked in a distillery before Prohibition. After some recent trouble with the law (which he kept a secret), he decided that it would be better to work with a smaller, out-of-the-way still. He left the big-time, gangster-run bootleg operation, but he brought his underworld sources of supply to my father's new business.

I always asked myself where and how my father managed to meet all the strange people he gathered about him. How did he manage to find a man familiar with the methods of distilling whiskey when conducting that business was against the law? You couldn't advertise for such a person. Where did he meet all those men?

Eddie arrived and departed only late at night. He drove his dilapidated truck into the driveway and unloaded supplies to the basement through the side door. I never saw him in daylight. He paid little attention to any of us, but occasionally he would bring me a trinket or candy.

First he would ask, "Have you been a good little girl?"

I always nodded and said, "Yes."

He would pull a bar of candy or a ball or two from his jacket pocket with a different explanation each time.

"I brought this for a good girl, and you're the first one who said yes, so this must be for you."

My mother never liked Eddie, and questioned why he was so nice to me. She never left my side when he appeared.

"Another bum," she would say. "A house full of bums, jailbirds, no-goodniks you bring here," she yelled at my father.

That was her constant refrain. My father ignored her outbursts or walked out, angering her more. Occasionally, exasperated, he would yell back, "Do you want to eat? Do you want a roof over your head? This is the only way. Stop *cheppering* me." He would walk out, returning later with a bunch of flowers or some other little peace offering for her.

One morning, I came downstairs early. I heard voices coming from the sunporch. One voice was my father's; the other I didn't recognize. I pushed aside the sheer curtains on the French door leading to the porch. I heard an angry voice tell my father that this was "a last warning." A stranger in a black pinstriped suit was pushing my father against the wall. He kept poking my father with his finger, punctuating each threat with a jab. He looked like Jack LaRue in all the gangster movies. I pushed open the door. I was very thin and pale, and in my nightgown and robe I looked emaciated. My dad pulled me to him.

The man acknowledged my presence. "This yuh kid?" he asked.

My father nodded. "My little one. There's a big boy, too."

The gangster changed his tone, dropping his voice to a conversational level. "Fer her sake, yuh shoulda keep yuh nose clean. The deal we got, yuh do the stuff an yuh make da booze—but only fer frens an like that. Small stuff. Big stuff, like case, yuh tell me. We take care a dem. Y'unnerstan?"

I thought he was finished, but he only stopped talking long enough to catch his breath. He continued to press his point. "Yuh don sell speaks. Yuh don sell clubs. Yuh don sell nobody what wants cases. If yuh don listen yuh gonna dig yuh own grave. What will happen to yer kids den?"

Terrified, I hid behind my father. The man continued, this time involving me in his threats. "Kid, don let yuh pa fuhget what I jus said."

My father drew me closer. He appeared calm, but his face was white and his hands tight, his fingers digging into my shoulders.

"Look," he said, "if I was really making money with my still, do you think my kid would look like this?"

The gangster stepped away and took a good look at me. Convinced, he mumbled, "Okay, okay. Y'made yuh point. Just make sure yuh keep it small. Only bottles, no cases for sale. Only sell around here. If we catch yuh selling cases to clubs, we'll be back." Now he looked like Eduardo Ciannelli threatening to bring in his whole mob, à la Hollywood. What did my plain, honest father have to do with this man? The man reached into his trouser pocket, pulled out a twenty-dollar bill, and put it into my father's hand.

"Here," he said, "get the kid some food and fatten her up." He left by the side door.

I was told to go upstairs and get dressed, and as I left, my father added, "Don't tell Mama!" I thought how fortunate it was at times like this that my mother was deaf. She wouldn't worry. I would!

ROSEDALE AVENUE

$\mathcal{I}$ never discussed my father's business with anyone. I often wondered why I alone knew these secrets. Why was I to keep this information from my mother? My father hinted at dire consequences if my mother knew of his plans. I never questioned his reasons; it was sufficient to hear him say, "Don't tell Mama. She would be very upset." I was not going to be the one to do that, for I vaguely knew that the word "upset" was an understatement.

I wanted to talk to my grandmother, to ask her the reason for hiding things from my mother. I was afraid that this might cause her pain, and intuitively did not want her to be angry with my father, but I finally questioned her.

My grandmother hesitated. She tried to put her thoughts

together to make her answer as revealing as possible without hurting the image I had of my mother.

She began, "Your grandfather and I loved all our children, but your mother was Grandpa's special child. He took her for walks; he took her to shows when I couldn't go for some reason. He never lied, but he told white lies when he bought her a blouse or a dress, saying that he got the sample from the factory for nothing. She was the apple of his eye. She could do no wrong. Didn't she have *goldeneh* hands like me, copying hats from expensive stores as a sample for her millinery company? Grandpa was so proud of her. She loved him so much.

"When she was twenty years old she went to Rockaway Beach one summer to help her aunt Hannah in her boarding house. Grandpa said she would be a help to his sister Hannah while she 'got a little sun and ocean.' While she was in Rockaway her papa took sick. It was double pneumonia. In two days he was dead. He died on a Thursday. Jewish law said he had to be buried before sundown on Friday.

"Your mama was coming back home Friday, so we did not want to tell her over the phone. She came home on Friday just when the hearse came to our house. Neighbors gathered on the stoop. When they saw your mother they shook their heads and some looked away. She joined them in sympathy and asked one woman, 'Who died?' Realizing she didn't know, they closed in around her. The woman answered, 'Your *tatteh.*' Her father. Your mama collapsed, and the neighbors carried her up three flights of stairs to our apartment.

"I tried to help her, but I was in shock, too. Your mother threw herself on the coffin and stayed that way until the men came to carry the coffin downstairs. At the cemetery she screamed, 'Papa, Papa, don't leave me, don't leave me!' Your uncle Benny stopped her from jumping into the grave with the coffin.

"Your mama never got over it. A few weeks later she was very sick with a high fever. The doctor told us it was a brain fever; he wasn't sure she would live. She slowly got better but it was a long time until she could talk or hear. All she ever said was 'Papa, Papa, why did you leave me?' over and over again. The doctor said the illness caused nerve problems; she was left hard of hearing.

"All these years she's still crying for her papa. She has a case of nerves. So we all take care not to cause any more big upsets to shock her. So *mamaleh*, you too have to take care not to upset your mother."

I finally understood why we were so careful around my mother. I remembered how I dreaded the Jewish holiday of Yom Kippur each year. From the moment that my mother lit the *Yaerzeit* glass, the memorial candle, on *Kol Nidre* until we broke fast the next night, my mother locked herself in the bedroom and sobbed and cried loud enough to be heard throughout the house. Reliving the day of my grandpa's funeral she cried out, "Papa, Papa, why, why? I need you, I miss you. Why? Why?" In one second, years before, my

mother had lost her father, her best friend, and her anchor in
life, and she never got over the tremendous loss.

So, reversing the role of mother and daughter, I continued to protect my mother from my father's misadventures,
but not with any peace of mind.

I had never spoken to my brother about my fears, although my father's pact with me to keep things from my
mother did not exclude my brother from knowing the goings-
on. But this time I was too fearful to keep it to myself. When
I related the event to my brother, he did not seem to be troubled by the story.

With a surprising degree of sympathy he said, "Listen,
Sis, don't make a mountain out of a molehill. That guy was
just trying to scare Pop. Pop shouldn't get mixed up with that
kind, but he can take care of himself. Sure they mean what
they say, but they got much bigger problems than Pop and
his little business. Don't worry."

Someone else telling me not to worry. How could words
stop me from conjuring up the vivid pictures my imagination
drew—my father lying in a pool of his own blood from bullet
wounds. Didn't gangsters kill people all the time? Weren't
there newspaper headlines and pictures of people murdered
every day? Why would my father be treated differently from
the others who crossed the mob? I mentioned these thoughts
to my brother.

Trying to reassure me, he said, "Those are just movie-type
gangsters. Big-shot gangsters against other big-shot crooks

when they're double-crossed. Pop is a little guy—hardly worth anyone getting into trouble over."

"But you weren't there," I cried. "He was pushing Daddy, threatening him. He warned him that if he didn't do what he said, he would be in real trouble."

"Okay, okay, but it ended good. Didn't it? The man turned out to be nice. Right?" my brother answered.

I tried to protest, but he interrupted. "So stop your worrying. Pop will do what he wants to do. Your worrying him won't stop him. You don't see Pop afraid, do you? So just stop! And for God's sake, don't worry Mama." Mac turned and walked out the door with his cut-down broomstick and catcher's mitt to join his friends in a three-sewer-cover gutter stickball game. Mac was not going to worry about anything but making a home run. I pondered whether my brother was worried or even concerned about our family affairs. If he was, he never spoke of it.

Aside from my father's business associates, we had a steady stream of refugees visit us on Rosedale Avenue. How were all these people who came all the way from Europe able to find us in the Bronx? Some were distant relatives, others were friends from the old country. After all, we were rich. We had our own house (mortgaged and now foreclosed, but more about that later), several bedrooms, a living room, a dining room, a sun parlor, and a backyard—all for a family of four. These people measured wealth by space, and we had space, space enough to house them for short visits—at least.

Some visitors dragged out their visits until my mother

prodded my father to "give them their walking papers." I
never knew most of their names. They were usually referred
to as the greenies, short for greenhorns, a name given to immigrants who had recently arrived at Ellis Island. My mother
distinguished each greenie by a physical or geographic description. There was the greenie from Budapest, and his wife
with the *fakrimpte fuss*—crippled legs. There was another
greenie from Budapest who was distantly related to my father, so distantly that my father could not get the relationship
straight. One visitor cried all the time, wishing to be home
with his family in Hungary.

They filled our house, ate whatever food we could share,
and drove my mother into a frenzy. She finally halted the
stream of traffic by putting her foot down, declaring, "My
home is not a hotel. If you want them to stay here, I'll make
it a hotel for pay!" My father knew that when my mother was
fed up you had to placate her or her temper would boil over.
The flow of visitors ceased for a while.

Short visits to our house ended. No more greenies. After
several months, my father announced that his uncle, aunt,
and cousin had arrived from Austria. They would stay with us
for a little while. My mother reluctantly accepted the idea,
telling my father to keep his promise of "just a week or so."
Uncle Jerome, Aunt Helen, and Barney moved into the third
bedroom upstairs. My brother and I reluctantly shared my
room.

Uncle Jerome was a Prussian dictator. He took over his
room, commandeered his family and eventually the entire

house as if we were living with him. His harsh, guttural voice barked out orders and demands like a German general. He put us on a schedule of exercises, tasks, and mealtimes, and he even dictated diets and menus. My mother objected, my father ignored him, I stayed away from him, but his presence dominated our lives. What little food we had was shared. Whatever food he brought in he selfishly took up to their room. The few weeks became months, and finally a year.

At last, Jerome found a job as a freelance photographic retoucher. He would place the portrait negative on a light box and with special photographic equipment and a sharp, pointed stylus, he'd retouch blemishes on the negative, straightening a bump on a nose, removing a wart, unwrinkling a heavily lined face, until the new negative became that of a handsomer or prettier face, not the original.

When he finished he'd say, "They say photographs don't lie. Ha! That's America. Everything is a lie here." Then he'd go off on another one of his anti-American tirades. Naively I wondered why he left his beloved Austria to live at our house.

I later discovered that he was also a fine artist, but his idea of an artist was someone who was soft and lazy; it was not a profession for a real German. A hobby, yes; a profession, no!

Aunt Helen stayed in her room mothering Barney. Barney was born to his parents quite late in their lives. Helen was in her forties when he was born. Uncle Jerome was twelve years her senior. Barney treated his parents as if they were his grandparents, very often reluctant to introduce them to his new friends. Maybe he was ashamed of them?

They stayed on and on. Eventually I became friends with Barney. His parents never seemed more than boarders who lived under our roof without contributing anything to our family or our daily life. Uncle Jerome never accepted us, our way of life, this country, or the times in which he lived. He longed for his home in Hungary, the bygone days of Strauss waltzes, rich pastries with *schlag* (whipped cream), Emperor Franz Josef, and gypsy violins. He refused to believe that the waltzers were becoming goose-stepping anti-Semites. "What used to be" was his constant refrain.

My mother would say sarcastically, "If it was so great, why did you leave?"

Whispering to my brother and me, she would add, "Why does he stay here? How did they find us? Did they look up Albert Kellerman, America, in a telephone book?" Her patience at an end, she would look up at the ceiling and cry, "How long, O Lord, how long?"

The invisible sign over our door which read WELCOME—OPEN DOOR attracted four-legged strays as well. Little dogs, big dogs, mutts, and abandoned pedigreed dogs, the lame and the healthy, all appeared at our doorstep to share whatever leftover food my mother could scrape into a bowl and leave at the side door of our house. Despite her protests, a few of the dogs became boarders and, like my relatives, their short stays grew longer and longer until a few of them became members of the family.

Rex was a large black and gray German shepherd who wandered into our house to beg for food and returned day after day, sensing he would not be turned away without some morsel and a pan of cool water. When winter came and the temperature hovered near zero, my mother's heart melted. "Let the dog in. He'll sleep in the basement. What he eats outside he can eat inside." As much as my brother and I loved Rex, he knew that he belonged to my mother. His sad eyes followed her wherever she went. When my mother was unaware of our presence, we saw Rex, his head on her knees, being stroked by mother as she murmured, "Good boy, Rex. Good boy." Rex reciprocated by licking her hands. His sad eyes were full of love for this lady who gave him a home.

Beauty, part German shepherd and part some other kind of dog, was really my dog. Beauty followed me home from school one day. He was tan and brown with a beautiful white diamond-shaped mark along his snout and head. His soulful eyes captivated my mother. If we could share our food with Rex, Rex could learn to share his good fortune with Beauty, my mother reasoned. The two dogs got along fine. There was no competition between them. Rex had my mother; Beauty was secure with me.

Beauty watched over me like a mother hen. He walked me to school each day, snarling at anyone who came near me. He screened my friends, watching their actions, misunderstanding their pranks, until he finally accepted them and became their friend, too. My mother told me that Beauty could tell time. At a quarter of three he'd paw at the door to attract my mother's attention. She would open it and watch him as he raced down the street in the direction of my school several blocks away. When I came out, there was Beauty, sitting near the door of my classroom, scanning the movements of all the children until I appeared. Then he came to my side, licking my hands and my face. As if we were on a schedule, he would start in the direction of our house, looking back to check that I was following, trotting home.

One winter day I came out of school, looked at Beauty's regular waiting place, and found he was not there. After waiting a few minutes, I joined my friends to walk home along the barely plowed, snow-laden streets. Where could Beauty be? My mother was at the door. Before I could ask, she questioned me. "Did you see Beauty? I haven't seen him all day." Beauty was gone forever. We never knew what happened to him. I cried for days. Was he living with someone else or—I didn't even want to think it—was he dead?

While I was in mourning for Beauty, Willie (so named by my cousin Barney), a tan and white collie, arrived at our door. Thinking that Willie would ease my hurt and dry my tears, my mother allowed Willie to become another canine boarder. Willie didn't become my dog. He belonged to all of us—his loyalty was to the last hand that fed him. Willie and Rex coexisted. They were totally indifferent to one another, or so we thought—until, to our amazement, Willie grew fat

on his meager diet of table scraps. The fat was camouflage—
Willie was pregnant.

The first thing we did was change his name to Nellie and
the pronoun *him* to *her*. As the time of the delivery grew
near, my mother prepared a large corrugated cardboard carton with an old pillow and worn-out towels and placed it near
the warmth of the furnace, all to help Nellie give birth. Nellie had her own idea, when the time came. I heard my
mother scream, "Oh no! Not here!" I raced up the stairs to
our bedrooms. My mother came out of hers and hurriedly
closed the door. I heard Nellie crying and whining. My
mother told me to go back to the kitchen. As she rushed
around upstairs, I sat on the steps listening and looking up.
Nellie's cries frightened me. I watched my mother tear up old
sheets. I couldn't imagine what was happening. I knew that
the story of the stork bringing human babies was a lie, but I
had no idea what really happened. How were dogs born? I
learned one fact: birth was painful. I wished Nellie would
stop howling. Finally, the noise was over. My mother told me
I could come up and see the puppies. There, in the center of
my mother's eyelet bedspread, were Nellie and her six puppies. Not all were tan and white. Some were gray and black
like Rex. Five of the puppies were healthy. Later, I heard my
mother tell my father that one was stillborn.

Nellie snarled when I approached her family. Her protec-
tive instinct came into play. She would not let anyone touch
her babies—even the dead one. My mother brought up milk
and food. Nellie trusted mother. Only she was allowed near

the puppies. The large carton was brought up to my mother's bedroom. Eventually, Nellie was coaxed into the box, carrying all six puppies by the scruff of their necks to their new bed. A day later, my father took the dead puppy away and hid it in the trash can's ashes. That night we saw the ash-covered puppy back in Nellie's box. Nellie had sniffed around the house until she found her missing baby. She stood guard over the box, and her eyes seemed to be counting and recounting her children all the time. Her recuperation was fast. In days she was bounding down the stairs to her favorite room—the kitchen—in search of more morsels of food.

The next time, my father buried the dead puppy far from our house. Nellie went hunting, but never found it. It was hard for her to feed all those hungry mouths. Nellie's milk supply was scarcely adequate to nurse her pups, but within weeks of their birth, my father had found good homes for four of the five. I was allowed to keep one male puppy. Each time my father placed a puppy in a neighbor's home Nellie would fetch it back to the carton. My mother discoursed on mother love. If Rex was the father, he showed no concern for Nellie or her babies. My mother discoursed on that, too.

After a month of this routine, the puppies were allowed by Nellie to remain in their adoptive homes, and if Nellie and her children chanced to meet on the street from then on, there was barely any recognition of their relationship or even their mutual existence. Dog motherhood was strange, I thought.

I never again believed all the myths of birth. I knew that

it was a painful experience and I did not know why adults called it beautiful. What I had seen was more like a bloody mess—and right on that beautiful snowy-white bedspread too. The miracle of birth remained a secret to me—nobody would tell me how the puppies came out of Nellie's body, and certainly nobody told me how they got in there in the first place.

Nellie died that winter pursuing her favorite sport—chasing cars and barking at their tires. Nellie was killed when she was dragged by a car; she was caught in its tire chains.

Rex lived out his life peacefully, but there was one time he got himself and us into a nearly disastrous situation. The basement windows had bars on them to ward off burglars and snoopers. Rex rarely went down to the basement, but during the hot summer months, it was the coolest place in the house. One Saturday, when we were visiting my grandmother, Rex pushed the basement door open and took refuge on the cool concrete floor. Thirsty, he lapped up the contents of a bowl left on one of the tables. Neighbors saw and heard him howling; he tried to escape from the basement through the barred windows. His head got stuck between the bars, and he howled for hours. Luckily, my father returned home before the police were called. He went for his friend Nick, and Nick came with some of his special tools. My mother and I returned home just as Nick was sawing a second iron bar to release Rex's head and thus stop his howling.

When Rex saw my mother, his yelps turned into plaintive whines. She lashed out at my father. "This is going to be the death of me. Even the dogs are in trouble."

My father tried to make a joke of it. "I didn't know Rex was a lush."

My mother didn't think it was funny. She went on about its being a near disaster.

"What if someone called the cops? What would happen then? You wouldn't make jokes." She spent her anger on what-ifs, and she tended to poor drunken Rex by putting a cold wet towel on his head. He went back to the kitchen and lay under the table to sleep it off. My mother sat with her head in her hands foretelling what might have happened *if.*

For me, these were the simple times—times of clear divisions: right and wrong, rich and poor, and black and white, bad to be punished, good to be rewarded. But I soon began to see a gray area somewhere in between. How could I explain my father? He was a good man, kind to everyone, unable to say no to those who asked for his help. But his way of life was against the law. He loved us, but he made my mother cry much of the time. My mother said that he was as crooked as the bums he associated with in our basement. Yes, my father was a good man, but he was doing something bad by breaking the law. I told myself that what he was doing had to be right—or at least it was in his case. After all, my father could do no wrong. I had to rationalize his behavior. I had to fix the blame. It had to be the terrible Depression—even if I had little understanding of what that meant.

FAMILY TIES

Saturdays were a contrast to the daily excitement on Rosedale Avenue, but they were also very special. Every Saturday morning my mother and I boarded the Soundview trolley, transferring twice to arrive at our destination, my grandmother's apartment on the Grand Concourse. When I was pressed by relatives to name my favorite person in the whole world, I would usually name my parents, but secretly I knew that the true answer was my Grandma Lubin. I was her favorite, and she let me know it.

"Do you know why the sun comes out each day?" she'd ask.

"No," I'd say and wait for her usual answer—happily.

She would hold me on her lap and say, "To shine on you, of course!"

We went through this verbal routine every week, and then she kept me enthralled with her wonderful stories of the olden days in Poland.

She was born in the city of Lodz in Poland, one of two daughters of a middle-class merchant. Lutka was the baby in a family of four children. Her father believed, as most Jews did, that the most important possession a Jew could have was an education. It was said that a job, land, a home, jewels, and clothes could be confiscated by the government, but what you learned and kept in your head could never be taken away. Her brothers learned the *Talmud Torah* for their bar mitzvahs in a *chedar*, but were also sent to a Polish school to learn languages, mathematics, history, and science. And as an enlightened parent, her father also sent Grandma to school to study with her brothers. It was unheard of in those days. In addition to the household skills she learned from her mother, Grandma was taught to read, write and do simple mathematics, and even learned several languages.

When word came to Lodz that her two brothers were to be conscripted as privates into the Polish army despite their education, the family decided on an alternative. The two young men would go to Hamburg, Germany, and board a ship that would take them to America to pursue a better life.

Anti-Semitism, always present in Poland, grew worse in bad economic times when crops failed and businesses closed down. Always the scapegoats, Jews were once again the victims of a purge. The pogrom, the fear of every Jew, became the way of life in Lodz. Those who had land were driven off it, losing all possessions. Others were turned into the streets. Some were killed by the Cossacks riding their horses into escaping crowds, stomping and slashing homeless victims as they fled. Grandma and her parents escaped the tragedy, but her parents died of pneumonia a short time after they had left Lodz seeking a safer place. Her older sister thought that Lutka could have a better life with their brother Wolff in America. He lived with his wife in a town called Waterbury, in a place called Connecticut, where he had a job on a newspaper. Wolff sent the fare to Grandma to book passage from Hamburg, Germany, to New York City, America. On the ship she dreamed of her new home where the streets were paved with gold, where you could live in any town unafraid of late-night raids by the Cossacks. Filled with the dreams and fears of a new land and new life, she landed at Ellis Island in 1861, carrying a carpetbag with her clothes and a cardboard box of remembrances of Poland.

Grandma told me about those early days in New York City and Waterbury. When she became aware of her sister-in-law's hostility, she came back to New York City. There she lived with her older brother, Ben, until he decided to cross the country to seek his fortune in California. At the age of sixteen, she was alone in a big city, with her small family far away. While mastering the English language and the ways of her new country, she put her domestic skills to work as a cook, a baker, a waitress, and finally a seamstress, altering dresses by adding lace, beads, or embroidery. Sometimes she made the entire dress from a pattern, adding her own ideas to the design. She longed to use her more formal education, but found no job opportunities for a Polish woman.

Grandma answered an advertisement of a dress manufacturer for seamstresses—piecework for women sewing dresses together. Grandma graduated from hems and seams to embroidery and appliqué, each better paying but still piecework. When the presser, Max Lubin, saw her work, he told the boss that he would like to meet the girl with the "*goldeneh* hands." Grandma, in turn, looked at the handsome man with the piercing blue eyes and knew that this was the man she dreamed of. A mutual friend introduced Max to Grandma. Grandma, an educated woman with great ambition and high hopes, married a simple, honest, handsome man who fulfilled all *his* dreams by marrying this wise, worldly woman. Since being a Jew had never been anything but a problem for Grandma, she had ignored her faith and she had never practiced the rituals of a kosher home. But her love for her orthodox religious husband changed her ideas. She took Jewish dietary instruction for keeping a kosher home, burying her old dreams and prejudices to become a good wife and mother.

One evening, when a neighbor died, she was horrified to learn that he was to be buried in the pauper's cemetery, potter's field. How could a Jew be buried without a religious service, with no words said over him, no one to mourn him, to lie forever among *goyim?* She joined a group to form the Jewish Free-Burial Association, going from neighbor to neighbor and storekeeper to storekeeper, soliciting money to establish a fund for decent Jewish burials in consecrated land. The organization became her lifelong passion, and she served as its president for the next twenty years. Everyone on New York's East Side knew this aristocratic-looking woman who badgered merchants and manufacturers for donations for her pet charity.

"A rich, uptown lady, slumming," they said of her. But Grandma was a poor Lower East Side lady from Rivington Street who could not deal with the sadness of death compounded by lack of money for a decent burial. When the Triangle Shirtwaist Factory fire took its toll of many young seamstresses, Grandma not only collected for the society but visited the bereaved families, bringing food and her good common sense to help them out of their tragic situation. My grandfather, who had no such social conscience, basked in Grandma's happiness as a social reformer and would counter criticism of her activities from friends by calling Grandma his American beauty with *goldeneh* hands and a *kliegeh Kopf,* a smart head.

Lutka never made her husband feel less than the number one person in her life. When he lost his job as presser, she pitched in beside her husband to keep her apartment building clean as a temporary janitor, in exchange for free rent. During the day she hauled pails of soapy water to clean the steps. At night, she would put on her best dress and Grandpa would dress in his best suit and together they would go to a meeting at the Free Burial Lodge to be admired as a handsome couple by all of the members.

She told and retold the stories of her arrival in America when Abraham Lincoln was president, of the death of my grandfather at an early age, of her life as a Jew in her native land. She spoke with pride of her five children, but mainly of her eldest son, who was a successful songwriter. Her eyes would mist with tears when she talked about a daughter who died at the age of four when the pharmacist mixed a lethal poison instead of her prescription by mistake.

Teasing my grandmother as I was so often teased by adults, I asked, "So was Uncle Sam your favorite child because he made you so proud?"

Grandma carefully explained, "A mother has no favorites. Each one is a favorite. Sam was my first born. With him I became a mother. We named him after my father. He was my favorite oldest son.

"Your mama, Bertha, came next. She was named for your grandpa's mother. She was my favorite Bertha.

"Pauline is closest to my heart because I had so little time with her. You know how she died. I cried when my mother died, when my father died, when my husband died. But you never get over crying when your child dies. It's not the way it's supposed to be. So Pauline holds a special place in my heart.

"Benny was next. He was always a problem in school, and at home. He needed me more. So Benny was my special son.

"Then came Irving. He was a sickly boy, always with colds and fevers. Sometimes he had pneumonia. He was the sweetest and the gentle one. Of all my children he loved me the most. He was my good son.

"Years after I thought that Irving would be my last child, I had Aunt Esther. She was my baby. I loved her so much because I was so much older when she was born and she made me feel young again. My favorite *young* daughter.

"So now you know who my favorite was. All of them in a different way. Now don't ask me who my favorite grandchild is," she said with her knowing smile.

My grandma. Philosopher. Solomon. All-knowing, all-loving, all-wise Grandma. Most of her pleasures were centered in the lives of her grandchildren.

"My profit," she would say, with a smile.

Every Saturday I would visit her and sit at her feet listening to her stories. During school vacations, I went to see her during the week and got instruction in sewing, crocheting, knitting, and especially baking. First, I would watch her kneading the dough, forming the oval-shaped challah, braiding the dough for the twist, and finally brushing its top with egg white to make it shine. Then I was allowed to make a miniature challah all by myself. Grandma always baked and cooked much too much for her own consumption so that we could take food home to our house—a game she played each Saturday to help us out without bruising my mother's pride.

My mother's unmarried sister, Esther, adored us and treated us as if she were our other mother. She was given an allowance by my uncle since she lived with and cared for my grandmother. She always brought us some new clothes for the Passover or Rosh Hashanah holidays, and toys for Channukah.

My uncle Sam, the songwriter, would visit on Saturdays, bringing all sorts of food from Lindy's, Barney Greengrass, and the Tip Toe Inn, his regular haunts. We would get our share of lox, herring, and sturgeon, plus Grandma's baked goods to take home. These food packages kept my family afloat from week to week. Even when all sources of our meager income dried up, when many of our neighbors were hungry, there was usually food in our house, thanks in large part to the leftovers from my Saturday visits to Grandmother's house. We were not allowed to accept money from anyone, not even relatives, but my uncle would always give me a twenty-dollar bill, saying, "Take your mother home in a cab." This game my mother allowed, reasoning that her rich brother was providing a luxury, not a necessity. We never took a cab, pocketing this windfall for the weeks ahead. We were also allowed to take change from my uncle. He would tell us that we could have all the coins that were weighing down his pockets. My brother and I would rush out of the room to count the coins that we were given. At times we had fourteen or fifteen dollars to count. My uncle would change bills into coins for this charade, and it was played out a few times a month.

Uncle Sam became prosperous as a lyricist, having been a founding member of ASCAP, an organization that protects songwriters by guaranteeing payment of royalties for sheet music, records, and the use of the song on radio or in motion pictures. He plugged his music in stores, where a singer accompanied by a pianist would introduce his song and sell the sheet music. As did other composers, lyricists, and entertainers, Uncle Sam changed his Jewish name. He wrote all his music under his new name, Sam M. Lewis.

Uncle Sam induced well-known performers to sing his songs at cabarets, vaudeville, revues, or on radio programs. Often he was asked to become a "play doctor," to fix a shaky show by adding additional lyrics, writing comedy skits, or giving the performer his idea of how a song should be sung. I heard time and again how he worked with Al Jolson, getting him to get down on his knees when he sang "Mammy." In his role as a play doctor, he became friends with Jolson, Eddie Cantor, Jimmy Durante (who was part of a vaudeville trio), and Sophie Tucker.

On Christmas Day, dressed in our best, we all went downtown to my uncle's house on Central Park West to partake of a non-kosher family feast. Hattie, the black housekeeper, loved both the children and my grandmother, and she would cook for a week in preparation for this day. The dining table was heaped with food—turkey, glazed ham, sweet-potato pie, salads, breads and rolls, and pies, cakes, and cookies. On a smaller table were Nova Scotia lox, sturgeon, sablefish, herring, deviled eggs, and tomatoes for Grandma to eat, so she could observe her dietary laws. My uncle's wife was born an Irish Catholic but converted to Judaism, but she did not keep kosher. Grandma would not eat *traif.* She ate her fish, salad, and eggs from a special glass plate set aside for her use whenever she visited her son.

She secretly enjoyed this day as much as her grandchil-

dren. She would marvel at the tree with its beautiful orna-
ments and loads of brightly wrapped presents. We ate all day
and opened packages for hours. There were many practical
gifts—sweaters, scarves, gloves, robes, and the like—but also
a good share of games, toys, and books. Every year I would
get a new Effandbee baby doll, even after I was much too old
to play with dolls. Every year my brother would get another
baseball bat, glove, and football.

My uncle Sam told my grandma about his new song and
recited the lyrics to her. She beamed as he said them, and
her eyes became moist with pride. Her other son, Irving, sang
a favorite song—"My Yiddishe Mama." My aunt Molly played
many of Uncle Sam's songs on his piano and we joined him
in singing "Mammy," "Dinah," "Sitting on Top of the World,"
"For All We Know," and many others of *his* famous songs.
Grandma was the happiest woman I ever knew. She had her
children, her grandchildren, and her wonderful memories,
and she shared them with me, allowing me a glimpse of times
gone by and a feeling of belonging to a family stretching from
the Bronx to Poland.

These Saturday visits to Grandma and the annual Christmas were the highlights of my childhood, almost dimming
memories of the lean days in between.

THE KELLERMAN CLAN

On Sundays I would visit my grandma Kellerman with my father. My brother refused to go. My mother did not like her mother-in-law and rarely accompanied us. My father's mother was born into an aristocratic Austrian family and never forgot it. (She never failed to mention that in those days her homeland was known as the Austro-Hungarian Empire, and she placed special emphasis on the word "empire.") She married a rich landowner, a relative, and bore him fourteen children, nine of whom lived to maturity. In Europe, the children were cared for in infancy by a wet nurse and then a governess.

A story was told by several older siblings about my father's childhood to illustrate my grandmother's lack of maternal instincts. When my father was a three-year-old, times were bad, crops had failed, and outside the large estates, like my grandfather's, peasants were near starvation. The Magyars, roving gypsies, went from town to town seeking food and clothing. They came to Grandfather's farm to beg, and when they were turned away, they took their revenge by kidnapping a child and holding him for ransom. The price of freedom for a child was usually a cow, a few chickens, and a sack of grain. My father was the hostage. My grandma was heavy with her seventh pregnancy—my father was her fourth—while the wet nurse was still busy with the sixth child. The governess had more than her share of work, and so nobody seemed particularly concerned about my father's whereabouts.

When my grandfather received the ransom message, delivered orally by another gypsy, his reply was no. He did not deal with gypsy lowlife. He demanded my father's return, with no ransom paid, and sent the messenger away with dire warnings of what would happen to them if my father was not returned—immediately!

The kidnappers were starving gypsies, not criminals. They saw the logic of returning my father, since all he represented to them now was another mouth to feed. They sent him back to his family.

As incredible as the story sounds, it is true, and those familiar with the area, the times, and the gypsies knew it to be an ordinary event. I could not comprehend a mother who was not directly involved with her small children, nor a father who would not pay such a simple ransom for the return of his son. My father laughed whenever the story was told. He vaguely remembered his short stay with the gypsies and said, "They probably took me home fast because I was such a pest." My grandparents left Europe to escape anti-Semitism and their sons' army conscription, but Grandma Kellerman never acknowledged the United States as her home or English as her language. Even though she could read and write English fluently and read *The New York Times* every day, she never spoke the language, communicating in German or Hungarian.

She treated her sons, two of whom were born in the United States, with varying degrees of respect in direct relation to their financial status. The daughters were unmarried and treated with annoyance as unwanted burdens. Still, the large Victorian house on Hoe Avenue in the Bronx was fun to go to when my many cousins were there. Sliding doors separated the living room from the spacious dining room. We played "elevator" with the sliding doors or played outside in the gazebo or back barn. During the Depression, my father lost favor with his mother. Despite the size of the dining room table, my brother (who only went to holiday dinners at Grandma's house) and I were sent to eat in the kitchen while our cousins sat with their parents in the dining room. If it bothered my father, he chose to say nothing. I was hurt by his lack of anger, but realized that my father's sense of family loyalty would not permit him to criticize my grandmother.

The family business, wholesale paints and lacquers, was in financial difficulty. One married son had moved back to

Hoe Avenue, despite his wife's protestation. He and other members of the family at home at the time would play Monopoly endlessly. Two of Grandma's brothers also lived in the rambling house. They had a running chess game set up and quarreled over each move in what seemed like an everlasting struggle against boredom.

My mother never told her family the truth of our tenuous existence on Rosedale Avenue. My father's pride was even greater. Trying to keep up with his more affluent brothers, he would bring a little something to my grandmother every Sunday.

Dismissing the Depression as a figment of the country's imagination, Grandma Kellerman still had her meat and produce purchased and delivered from the most expensive butcher in the neighborhood. Her dreams of resuming her former way of life in the old Austrian Empire never died. Twice a year she summoned her dressmaker, who came to Hoe Avenue with her bolts of silks, satins, and laces, and cut a pattern for Grandma's new wardrobe. The style was always the same, and the fabrics were always the finest.

Twice a year at the holidays she acknowledged my existence by buying me a *yomtov* dress: a silk dress with smocking for Pesach (Passover), and a velvet one with a lace collar for Rosh Hashanah (New Year). My aunt Teresa would take me to an exclusive children's shop on Southern Boulevard for these dresses. She understood how I hated these dresses, which were not the style or fabric worn by my friends, but she told me that she could not fight Grandma. I wore each dress only once, to visit my grandmother in *shul* on the holidays. My dress and appearance were a reflection of her status, showing to all who saw her at the synagogue that I was granddaughter of a grande dame. I'm not sure which I disliked more, Grandma or the dress.

Teresa sympathized with my feelings toward my grandmother Kellerman. She would never publicly criticize her mother, but on this occasion she let me know how she felt about Grandma's rigid manner and the opinions and prejudices that caused constant friction between mother and daughter.

Teresa, a woman in her thirties, listened to everlasting criticism for owning and driving a car, working as a secretary/bookkeeper for a widower who owned an automobile repair shop, and especially her independent behavior. When my aunt added garage mechanic to her job (wearing pants as a requisite of the work), Grandma was furious.

Grandma worried about what people would think of a Kellerman woman behaving in an improper manner with an attitude of "It's nobody else's business what I do with my life!"

The last straw came when Teresa announced her intention to marry her boss. Grandma didn't attend the wedding, refusing to acknowledge the union and completely disowning Teresa. It was years before Grandma, at the urging of her other children, reluctantly allowed her daughter to visit the family home.

I finally convinced my father that I could not go to Hoe

Avenue every Sunday. He went alone, caught in a bind between his mother and me, hurt by both of us.

My brother, Mac, was never part of the family excursions.
He visited Grandma Lubin each week at whatever time
suited his teenage schedule. He never went to see his other
grandmother and probably never gave her a thought.

My brother was born five years before my arrival, the
firstborn child on both sides of the family. Named for our
maternal grandfather, Muttel (Max), he was the pride of the
Lubins, adored and spoiled for five years. As "crown prince,"
he could do no wrong. My mother thought that the universe
revolved around this bright little boy who could perform
marvelous feats of memory. He could identify my uncle
Sam's songs by the pictures on the sheet music and his Victrola records by the color of the label. He performed his act
for my uncle and his show business friends at parties at
Grandma's house to enthusiastic adult approval. I, on the
other hand, was not impressed by the show-business friends
my uncle brought with him to Grandma's house. Sophie
Tucker, Al Jolson, Eddie Cantor, Weber and Fields, and many
others had no idea how to relate to a little girl. They either
teased me or asked what I considered silly questions. But I
loved to hear them sing for my grandma. I had no idea how
famous my uncle was.

It should have come as no surprise to anyone that my
birth would be a great blow to my brother and his status in
his young life. He was no longer the only child of my parents,
and he also lost the title of only grandchild. I was resented

from the start, and he let everyone know it. As a teenager, his resentment toward me turned to tolerance and he became in-different to my existence. He was so absorbed in his life with his friends, sports, games, and *Doc Savage, Argosy,* and *Dime Detective* magazines that I was just a nuisance who lived un-der the same roof. At times, I was jealous of my brother, be-lieving that he was my mother's favorite, but secretly I admired his independent nature and looked up to him. I wished that he would pay more attention to me in a form other than shooting cardboard at my legs with his rubber-band gun.

One spring day he was asked—or probably bribed—by my mother to take me downtown to the Paramount theater to see *Cimarron* and a special stage show. We left our house early that morning, taking the Soundview Avenue trolley to the IRT subway station. The train started out elevated, riding past Elder Avenue, Simpson Street, Prospect Avenue, before going underground until we reached Forty-second Street. Times Square was the most exciting place I could possibly imagine. Its high buildings, many movie houses with lighted marquees, huge billboards, and trolley and car traffic that seemed to converge at one spot—all this left me spellbound. My brother walked me over to Forty-third Street to the Para-mount. At the box office he asked for only one ticket of ad-mission. I questioned him, but he said he didn't want to see the movie.

"It's a girl movie," he said. "I'm going to see a war movie.

Listen, I'll be right here when your movie ends. Stop crying. I'll get a nice lady to take you inside."

He asked a woman to walk me into the theater. "Don't forget," my brother said. "Wait right here at the end of the show. See you later."

The nice lady took me to a seat in the orchestra section. I looked around in awe. The Paramount was huge. The seats were red plush. The thick carpet was red and gold. The curtains and drapes were of a shiny gold fabric, and all around the auditorium gold paint framed archways, railings, and the side boxes. This was truly a palace. The gold curtain rose, the screen filled the stage, and I became totally engrossed in the movie *Cimarron*.

I never thought about my brother until the movie and stage show ended. When the lights went on, I followed the crowds to the exit. I went to the place where my brother had instructed me to stand, and I waited and I waited. I waited for some time before I became frightened. So many things could have happened to Mac in all that traffic. I waited. Finally, I cried. A Paramount usher dressed in a handsome black uniform, with a red satin stripe running the length of his trousers and a black cape lined in red, came over to talk to me. I told him that my brother was supposed to meet me to take me home. I was afraid that he might have been hurt in an accident. The usher, not much older than my brother, reassured me, telling me that Mac was probably late because "he just forgot the time."

"He'll be here soon," he said. "Don't worry."

Minutes became an hour. The usher called a passing policeman, who questioned me.

"What's the matter, little girl?"

I told him.

"How old is your brother?"

He nodded knowingly at my answer.

"Don't worry. Your brother's okay. Big brothers sometimes forget little sisters. Do you know your telephone number?"

"We don't have a telephone," I answered.

As frightened as I was, I didn't want anyone to call my mother to Mr. Wiener's telephone. Such a call was reserved only for emergencies. I remembered the shock and pain that accompanied such calls in the past when an aunt died and my father was called to the phone.

"Okay, don't cry," he said. "I'll take you home. Do you know where you live?" the policeman asked. I nodded. He took my hand.

"What about my brother? He'll be worried," I cried.

"Don't worry about him. He'll find his way home. He'll have a good excuse, you'll see," he said knowingly. He smiled at me and tried to make me smile. "Big brothers are all alike," he added.

My mother was waiting at the porch window, her usual spot when anyone in the family was late. When she saw me with a policeman, she ran out of the house to meet us on the sidewalk. Excitedly, she asked what happened.

"Are you hurt? Where's your brother? Why did a policeman bring you home?" she asked without allowing me to answer.

I tried to tell her but her eyes were riveted on the policeman. She thanked him and tried to get rid of him as quickly as possible.

"That boy of yours deserves a good licking, leaving his sister downtown all alone."

My mother didn't hear what he said, but said "yes" to the officer, taking my arm and guiding me toward the house.

"Wave good-bye and say thank you to the nice man," she said, and she waved too.

When we were inside the house she went back to her window post to make sure that the policeman had left the area. Then she sat down and cried. I sat on her lap and put my head on her shoulder. She put her arms around me. I felt so safe. "Your brother! When I get my hands on him I'll break his neck," she threatened.

She rocked me gently back and forth in her arms. Exhausted, but feeling much better, I went to my room. Mother waited impatiently on the porch, her anger increasing as the minutes passed.

Mac came home an hour or so after I did. He had rehearsed his story, embellishing it with fantastic details, on his long ride home. He decided on the offensive method of attack. I was to be the culprit. I didn't wait for him exactly where he had asked me to stand. The movie was over earlier than he had expected. An usher said that I had left earlier with someone. I sat through more than one performance. All these excuses were rehearsed over and over again until he decided which to use to convince my mother that he was blameless. With mock anger he stormed into the sun parlor yelling, "Where is she? I'll wring her neck. Never tell me to take her anywhere ever again!"

My mother was amazed at Mac's outburst. First she said nothing. Then she raised her hand and slapped him across the face.

She yelled, "What lies have you made up? A policeman had to bring her home. A policeman!"

She went toward my brother to hit him again, but this time he was able to dodge her blow and ran through the house, slamming French doors before my mother, in pursuit, could reach him. He ran out of the house, taking three steps at a time, jumping over the back fence to Noble Avenue and the farms beyond.

Mac didn't come home until it was dark; he even missed dinner. My mother, having spent her anger, was worried about my brother's whereabouts. When he came home, she put some food on a plate and waited for him to sit at the table. They both sat there in silence.

After a few minutes, my brother broke the silence by extending his hand toward my mother, mumbling, "I'm sorry, Ma. I'm really sorry."

My mother sighed and very quickly spoke to him. "I never ask you to do anything. Just this once I asked you, begged you, to do me a favor. I asked you this one time to take your sister to the movies."

My brother answered, "Well, I took her, didn't I? You asked me to *take* her. You didn't say anything about bringing her *back*."

My mother reached across the table. I was sure that she was going to slap him again. She raised her hand, but to our amazement, she began to laugh and laugh and laugh. My brother's excuse was so far-fetched that it was funny. But as she laughed, the laughter turned to tears. Through her tears, she explained not only her anger, but also her fear.

"Mac, don't you understand? You didn't bring your sister home. That was bad enough. You deserved a real beating for that. But you made a policeman bring your sister home. A policeman! What if he came in and smelled the liquor in the basement? What would have happened? Your father could go to jail!"

My brother went to my mother and put his arm around her. She melted. How she loved him. She forgave him.

"Now apologize to your sister. Irene, kiss your brother and forgive him."

We did as we were told.

"Goodnight, Sis. I'm really sorry about what happened today."

I went up to my room wishing that I could have told my brother how much I really loved him. Sisters did not tell their brothers such things. I kept my secret. But my mother told my father the events of the day when he came home late that night.

"A policeman was here," she said. "Here! One of these days there will be trouble. I feel it in my bones! You'll see. They'll be here and you'll go to jail. Wait. You'll see!"

It was a long time before my mother forgot that day. In time, we went back to our routine, visiting my grandparents, seeing our relatives, surviving the hard times in our small world in the Bronx.

THE PICNIC

*T*he cathedral-shaped Atwater Kent radio blared out the call for tallying the state delegates' numbers at the 1932 National Democratic Convention in Chicago on that hot July night. My father handed me a lined pad and several pointed pencils that he had sharpened with a paring knife and then scraped on a pad of sandpaper.

"Write," he said. "Put down all the states, starting with Alabama."

We waited for the roll call to begin. The chairman at the convention rapped his gavel several times and finally the noise abated. The chairman cleared his throat and in a flat monotone voice called, "Alabama." The delegate from Alabama rose and, after a lengthy description of the virtues of his state, yelled, "Alabama, the flower of the southland, casts its votes for the next president of the United States, Franklin Delano Roosevelt!" The convention roared its approval. My father, an immigrant from Hungary, felt the importance of each individual being a part of his new homeland—America. I was to learn about its government, how it worked, and how wonderful democracy was, starting now. I was nine and a half years old, going into sixth grade. My father watched me write the number of delegate votes next to the name of Alabama. He asked, "What is the capital of Alabama?" I shrugged my shoulders.

"How can a girl who was born in this country and who goes to school free in this country not know the capital of Alabama?" he asked, and sighed in disbelief.

He had had to learn these and many other facts as an immigrant to get his citizenship papers, but his child, born and schooled here, didn't know it. The convention was once again brought to order. "Arkansas," called the chairman. The delegate from Arkansas cast all its votes for Franklin Delano Roosevelt. And so it went far into the night, my father constantly interjecting his questions about each state as the votes were cast.

"Which is the most important city in California?" "What is the main industry in Pennsylvania?" "When did we purchase Louisiana?"

He took great pride in knowing which questions to ask. Unfortunately, my answers alternated between "I don't know" and "We didn't learn that yet." As the night wore on and the convention lasted longer than expected, my eyes began to shut.

My father took the pad and pencil, patted me on the head, and said, "If it's nice Sunday, we'll go on a picnic to Connecticut. Would you like that?"

"Oh, yes," I said. "I'll pray for good picnic weather."

My father kissed my forehead and sent me to bed. As I walked up the stairs, he called out, "What's the capital of Connecticut?"

"Oh, Daddy. Not now," I murmured and continued up the stairs. I had my own room on the second floor of our one-family house.

The Sunday of our picnic was a beautiful day, no clouds, a blue sky, a smell of fresh-cut grass, and a brilliant warm sun. Perfect! My dad suffered from epilepsy and was not allowed to drive a car because he never knew when an attack would come on suddenly, so Bill, our "chauffeur," checked out the big, black, seven-passenger Pierce-Arrow. The black car shone in the sunlight. All the chrome on the headlights, door handles, and trim were polished to a mirrorlike finish. Bill cleaned the upholstery and rubbed the same oil into the leather that my brother used on his baseball glove. The big black car was Bill's pride and joy—and he babied it like a child. He drove the car, made deliveries, raked leaves, shoveled snow, and did odd jobs that came up. In bad weather, he drove me the fourteen blocks to my school. He was one of the family. I took our car for granted, never questioning how we were able to own a car when we didn't always have enough food, and had to stuff newspaper in the soles of our shoes when a hole appeared. After all, my father needed a car to conduct his "business." It was a necessity of life.

Bill sang his favorite song, "Let Me Call You Sweetheart," as he put several heavy cartons on the floor in the back of the car, in place of the jump seats. The smell of honey-dipped fried chicken and hot biscuits rose to my bedroom. I ran downstairs, eagerly anticipating the next step in picnic preparations. My mother put free fruit from a nearby farm in a basket. Bill filled a thermos jug with hot coffee and glass milk bottles with lemonade. My mother got in and sat on one side of the backseat. Bill draped an old khaki blanket over the cartons on the floor, making a continuous bench across the floor of the car. This is where I sat. As usual, Mac was staying home to pitch a softball game on the block. My father and Bill got into the front seat and, after some sputtering and assorted noises, the car was on its way along Soundview Avenue.

We turned onto Westchester Avenue and finally onto Manor Avenue, where we stopped to pick up more passengers. My favorite person, my grandma, came slowly down the steps from her stoop carrying a carton of goodies. I smelled her butter cookies and apple pies, and she and the food became one marvelous feeling of good things to come. My aunt, my mother's younger sister, helped Grandma into the backseat and went around the car to sit on the other side of her. My little cousin climbed in and sat beside me on the blanketed cartons. Grandma, who was a huge woman, spread her skirt over the front of the cartons and told my father that we were ready to go. We started again. I looked around the car and thought that no day could be more perfect in all respects. I was going on a picnic on a beautiful day with the people I loved best in the whole world. What a lucky girl I was!

Preparations for this family outing had actually begun many weeks before this special July Sunday. Bill had driven over to my school several times to take me on shopping expeditions with him. We'd leave the four-room wood schoolhouse and drive to the South Bronx, where many junkyards were located. Bill talked to the owners and, before any money changed hands, we dug through mounds of glass bottles. Bill told me to choose carefully, to make sure the bottles were not chipped or cracked. They had to have narrow necks, and most important, for each size and shape we had to have twelve identical bottles. When we had filled cartons with the necessary bottles, I was allowed to rummage through another section of the yard to pick out bottles that pleased my childish idea of beauty.

And those bottles were so beautiful. They were of unusual shapes—short, squat, triangular, heart-shaped, hexagonal, with small wide mouths or long thin necks. They were tinted smoky gray or deep brown, pale green, amber, light blue, and even a rosy pink. I loved to hold these bottles up to the light and watch the area around me turn different colors. The bottles were dusty, but I could imagine how they would sparkle when they were washed in hot soapy water. Some bottles still had their original labels on them.

Bill bargained with the junkyard proprietor until an amicable agreement was made. Then he would put the cartons of purchased bottles in the back of the car, placing the well-worn blanket over them. After making several purchases at other yards and backyards of private houses, we drove home, pulling into the driveway next to our basement. We always returned home late enough not to be unloading the car in daylight.

When all the supplies except the bottles were in the basement, my father took over, telling each member of the family what to do. "Birdie," he'd say to my mother, "do the brown quart bottles first."

A large galvanized steel tub would be half filled with water and a dash of vinegar and finally the brown bottles were added. They boiled in the water on the gas range, the tub covering all four burners. After the water boiled for a while, the bottles were taken out one by one, all loose labels were removed and the bottles were rinsed in cool, clear water. This procedure was repeated, and then twelve sparkling clean bottles each were placed in a corrugated, compartmentalized carton. The cartons were brought down to the basement.

Bill's job was to mix some ugly granules with water in a tin can and place it on an electric one-burner stove. He stirred the contents of the pot constantly to prevent the resulting glue from burning. When the bottles were dry and spotlessly clean, labels were selected for each group of twelve. The labels read "Four Roses," "Old Overholt," "Green River," and other brand names of the day. Special labels with exotic names were used for the fruit cordials, and a German name was chosen for Kümmel brandy. My father had to please his ego by using something of his own name on some of the labels, so he introduced two new brands, "Princess Irene" brandy (named for me) and "Monogram" whiskey with his own design in black and gold and a label that stated, "A. Kellerman and Son, distillers since 1813." He established his trademark by putting forth his company as viable competition to name brands. In part, this was true. My father's family had owned grain farms for centuries, and as a by-product, they did distill liquor for limited consumption in Hungary.

The liquor for these bottles had been fermenting and filtering in large vats in our basement. It looked like a science laboratory with funnels connected to glass tubing itself connected to other funnels and spouts. Many different fruit and mash smells wafted upstairs when the cellar door was opened. There were always some bottles that were full. Other bottles were left empty while liquor aged longer in the vats. When all the bottles were filled, the cork was secured by a special label, a "government stamp" printed prior to Prohibition, and then further sealed with hot red wax and a stamper.

At this point, the order was almost ready. We had to get each carton labeled for the specific order, which usually came from a country club intent on fulfilling its members' desires to imbibe alcoholic beverages despite Prohibition. My father was what was commonly known as a bootlegger, but a little independent one, unknown to the law enforcers or the crime syndicates. This was his answer to unemployment and the Depression: he survived as a breadwinner, putting food in our stomachs and coal in the furnace. By 1931, several of our Italian neighbors were also in the wine-making business in their cellars. When asked, they said that they were making sacramental wines that were legitimately part of their religious rituals. My father rationalized that his *schnapps* was an important part of his cultural and religious affairs, like bar mitzvahs or weddings. Everyone except my mother thought that he was in the right.

After all the cartons were filled, some special ones were banded with thin metal strips, placed in burlap wrapping, and taken to the marshland near the Clason Point ferry slip, where they were lowered into the shallow salt water part of the sound. Then the burlap and cartons were allowed to dry in the sun in our backyard for several days. The order was finally ready for the "picnic." My father notified the country club that the boat had finally arrived with "quality stuff" for their members.

We drove along the highway reading Burma-Shave ads aloud, spotting cows and horses, laughing and singing while we sat on the cartons, the contents of which we had worked on for several weeks. I was happy in anticipation of this great picnic, ignorant of the dangers and risks of what we were doing.

By noon, we drove up to the Connecticut Country Club.

There was a uniformed attendant at the high wrought-iron gates. My father handed a letter to the man and we were directed through the gates to a curving, tree-lined driveway which led to a beautiful, well-kept Victorian mansion. A wide veranda banded the main floor. Flower beds and shrubs were everywhere; huge trees shaded the lush, green grass carpet. Well-dressed women in flowered voile dresses and large brimmed straw hats to shade their pale faces from the sun sat on the ornamental white iron benches. I guessed that they were rich people, and it was a wonder to me that they were not affected by the Depression. We drove past the wraparound veranda to a small side door at the rear of the mansionlike club.

Bill went into the house and came back with a very tall, well-groomed man who asked for my father. My father and the man talked for a few minutes while Bill removed the cartons from the car. A bottle was taken from the first carton, opened, and a small amount of whiskey was poured into a glass which the gentleman was holding. I watched him first sip the liquor and then swallow the rest in one gulp. He said nothing. He seemed deep in thought. My dad simply waited. Finally, the man said, "It's pretty good, but you've brought me better." My dad commented on the increased costs, higher risks, competition from the big boys, but said that he had also brought more expensive merchandise although he wasn't sure that the country club wanted to go higher in price. The man nodded. Bill brought out one of the burlap-wrapped, Long Island Sound–dipped cartons. The man's face showed immediate approval. Now he was getting what he wanted—real "Scotch."

"This looks like the real McCoy. Right off the boat. I can even smell the sea air," he said.

My father said nothing. Bill ceremoniously broke the official-looking seal, opened the bottle, and once again poured a small amount into another glass. This time the man began sniffing the contents, then sipped it slowly, rolled it around in his mouth until he swallowed the last drop. The expression on his face told all. He beamed.

"This is it! This is the real thing. I could tell as soon as I smelled the carton and saw the wrapping."

He and my father walked off, negotiating a deal. He bought all the burlap-wrapped cases, some bottles from the first cartons he had tasted, and the cartons of cordials and liqueurs in the beautifully tinted bottles for the ladies in the club. My father's day was a success; only one carton was returning with us. My day was just beginning.

We got back into the car and drove along the highway. I was sitting on the carton trying to figure out why the man thought the liquor from the cartons with the burlap tasted better than the other. It was all the same. Why did he pay twice as much for those bottles? Did my father deliberately fool him? The question crossed my mind, but I immediately dismissed the thought.

Bill turned off the road to a picnic area near a small lake. We laid claim to a table with long benches and unloaded the food from the car. The food tasted as good as it had smelled.

After we ate, my cousin and I took off our shoes and socks and went wading. Dad slept. Bill called us back and played catch with us. The ladies cleared the table and sat on canvas chairs, enjoying the sun. They had no hats to shield their skin from the burning sun. Unused to being idle, each of them had brought knitting or embroidery to do. "Idle hands are the devil's playground," Grandma warned.

When the sun went down, we reluctantly climbed back into the car to take the long drive back to the city. The women returned to the rear seat, but my cousin wanted to sleep, so she was made comfortable stretched across the length of the blanket, her back against the remaining carton. It had been a perfect day.

I sat between Bill and my father on the drive home. I fell asleep with my head in my dad's lap. I was startled awake by motorcycle sirens. I heard my father say to someone, "We were speeding because my daughter is ill, and we were rushing her to the hospital." I wanted to say, "Who's sick?" but my father's hand covered my mouth. The motorcycle policeman insisted on escorting us to the local hospital. When we reached the hospital, Bill picked me up in his arms and carried me inside. I was bewildered. My dad thanked the policeman and told him that he need not wait. Bill carried me through the hospital corridor and took me out the back way. He saw that the policeman had left and we got back into the car. He turned the car around and went in the opposite direction from the route of the motorcycle.

Finally I was able to ask, "Who's sick? What happened?"

My dad said abruptly, "No one!" His face was white. Why was that?

While I slept, Bill had been driving too fast. When we were stopped by the motorcycle policeman, my father remembered the carton still in the car hidden under the blanket. He looked down at me on his lap. My face was flushed and perspiring from the heat of the day. Again, my appearance came to my father's rescue. He told the policeman that I had fainted; hence, the escort to the hospital.

I guess all's well that ends well. The day was beautiful, the food delicious, the company my favorite people. My dad had a financially successful day. But when I thought of my father's ashen face, and the fear that I saw in my mother's eyes when I awoke, I never again felt quite safe. For the rest of my father's bootlegging days, I agreed with my mother, and waited for the ax to fall.

THE RAID

$\mathcal{M}$y mother never did accept the still in our basement. Despite the presence of similar illegal business on the street, my mother was certain ours would be found out and severe punishment would follow. Being deaf intensified her fears. If she saw neighbors looking toward our house, talking to each other, she was sure that they were discussing our family and the existence of the bottles and the liquor in the basement. The smell of the sour mash fermenting was enough to put terror in her heart. My father's attempts to reassure her fell on deaf ears.

Her anxiety grew when one of our neighbors was visited by two uniformed policemen one summer day. All activities on the block stopped. The boys froze in their gutter game of Red Rover; the men put down their newspapers or rakes and left their porches; the women came to their doorways. My mother retreated to the sun parlor and stood frozen at the window. Everything and everyone was still. Why were the policemen at the Ferraras' front door? Everybody knew of their wine-making in the garage, but many neighbors on the block were similarly engaged. Why this family? Who was the informer? The policemen went inside the Ferraras' house. The eerie quiet persisted for some time; then screams and hysterical cries broke through the silence. Mrs. Ferrara's wails resounded through the street. I was terrified and hid behind my mother, putting my hands over my ears to shut out the cries. Mrs. Ferrara's tortured cries sounded like her life was coming to an end. Other women in the house added their screams to her sobs. At that moment, I knew what the word "bloodcurdling" meant. "Giuseppe, Giuseppe mio!" she screamed over and over again. Finally, the door opened and Mr. Ferrara stepped out, followed by the two policemen. They were on either side of him and appeared to be holding him up. He looked helpless. His face and eyes were wet. His shoulders shook as he sobbed silently. The sobs and cries of the women behind him grew louder. A boy outside yelled, "It don't look like they pinched him." My father started across the street to see Mr. Ferrara, but Mr. Ferrara put up his hand as if to say "stay," and he came over to our side of the street. Between sobs he said, "It's not the trouble y'think. It's my Giuseppe, my Joey, he's dead." His sobs became convulsive; he could hardly talk.

"He fell down da elevator!"

He screamed in Italian, making a fist and thrusting it to-ward the sky.

"Why'd ya take my Joey, my Giuseppe, why?"

Some of the neighbors drew closer, others ran back to their homes. My mother was bewildered, unable to read lips at that distance. When I told her what had happened, she cried. She cried for Mrs. Ferrara and the family. She cursed the sky as Mr. Ferrara had just done, asking over and over again, "Why?" Then she worried about the whereabouts of my teenage brother and asked me to find him. Even though the policemen had come for a totally different reason, their presence made my mother fearful.

"It was an omen," she told my father, "an omen of bad things to come; you'll see."

This was my first encounter with the death of someone I knew. Joey, or Giuseppe as his mother called him, was a quiet young man who had left college when he was able to get a full-time job. Joey was the only bread-winner for the thirteen mouths to feed in the Ferrara household. He worked as a freight elevator operator at a factory in downtown Manhattan. He fell down the elevator shaft when someone forgot to put up the safety fence. Joey was the pride of his family. Not only did he work and bring money home each week, he was also the first Ferrara to attend college to become a lawyer. He was planning to return to college at night to get his degree when the accident occurred.

I was afraid to enter their house, but my parents brought field flowers and paid their respects. Joey was laid out in the

Ferrara living room. I couldn't believe that someone so young and healthy could die. "Why?" I cried.

The sky was overcast with promise of rain on the day of the funeral. One of my friends came over and we knelt near the sunporch windows to watch the proceedings. We had never seen a funeral before. A hearse and a car full of flowers and some black limousines were lined up along the curb. Father Paul and children from the Catholic high school went into the house. First a few older men came out; then Joey's six sisters. They were dressed from head to toe in black. Their heads were covered by black veils, which hid their red eyes. My friend Edith, with whom I most identified, almost fell down the steps. Her black garments made her appear so much older than her ten years. A young man broke her fall and she buried her face in his jacket. I cried out loud. How could this be happening to my friend?

When Joey's parents appeared, my mother began to sob, her heart aching for Mrs. Ferrara and all mothers who ever suffered the death of a child. Mrs. Ferrara came through the open door and sank to her knees. Joey's uncles tried to raise her. Finally, each took an arm and half carried her down the steps. The family stood near the hearse, making an aisle for the pallbearers and casket. Joey's friends were the pallbearers. The young men sobbed as they carried their friend down to the hearse. My friend Dotty and I cried out loud and hid our faces beneath the windowsill, unable to watch the tragic scene unfold. But Mrs. Ferrara's piercing screams brought us back to the windows. She was stretched across the coffin calling Joey's name and other words in Italian. Father Paul, a recently ordained priest and neighbor, put his arm around Mrs. Ferrara and whispered to her as he gently unfolded her from the casket and guided her to the first limousine. The family joined her, and the rest of the mourners took their seats in the other cars. The funeral cortege drove slowly down the street, around the corner, and out of sight.

The street became quiet. People left their windows, exhausted by the tragedy and the day's events. Even the boys, who were always on the street, remained indoors. The unusual silence was frightening. The block was in mourning.

I expected to have to pay a *shiva* call to the Ferraras after the funeral. My mother explained that Catholics have a wake before the funeral, and do not sit *shiva* after the funeral as the Jews do. I couldn't bring myself to cross the street to my friend's house, and was happy that a visit was not expected of me. Mrs. Ferrara did not appear outside her house until a few days later. She wore a black dress and a black shawl, and I never again saw her wear anything else. As a religious woman, she believed Joey's death was God's will and she was expected to accept it, but nevertheless she cried all the time.

The women thought as my mother did. They whispered to one another that it was God's way of punishing the Ferraras for their wine and whiskey business, because it was against the law. A few women made their husbands shut down the stills. My father ridiculed this kind of talk. He told my mother that carelessness, not God, killed Joey. I heard him yell that if there were really a God watching, he wouldn't have time to be vengeful against little law breakers, what with all the big-time bootleggers and gangsters running around loose.

"If God has so much time for nonsense, why doesn't he spend some of the time to end the misery we're in now?" he added.

I had never heard my father talk this way. He always told me that there was a God who was "mostly good." My mother was not convinced.

The Ferraras did penance. They closed down the wine barrels in the basement and garage, and the unpicked grapes died on the vines. Their dream of having their only son become a lawyer and returning in triumph to Italy died and was buried with Joey.

The street settled down into its usual routine. Only my mother seemed unable to forget the sight of the two policemen on either side of Joey's father. In a hushed voice, she told my father of her fear. My father shrugged it off as my mother's "nerves" and told my aunt that she would "snap out of it."

"An omen," my mother repeated. She couldn't shake her fears.

One afternoon her fear became a reality. As I rounded our corner of my street, I saw a car and a police van in our driveway. My father's uncle Jerome, who was living with us at the time, was arguing with a man in a dark suit. As I came to the stoop, I heard him say, "Let her ride in the car. I'll go in the wagon." Where was my mother going? She was always at home when we were expected from school. Then I saw a policeman with my mother. She was crying and kept repeating, "I knew it would happen. I told him I felt it in my bones." When she saw me she grabbed me and held me close to her.

The policeman told my mother that she would ride to the police station in the car, and Uncle Jerome was to go in the police van. But when Jerome saw my mother's face, he asked to sit with her in the car as well. While cases of liquor were put in the van, the detective wrote a name and address on a page in his pad, tore it out, and handed it to me.

"Little girl, give this to your daddy when he comes home," he said.

The paper had the precinct number, address, and phone number, as well as the telephone number of the bail bondsman. The two cars departed with my mother and uncle. I stood on the stoop becoming more and more hysterical. Mr. Wiener invited me to come into his house to wait until my father or brother came home. He tried to console me.

"They pull a raid on a still once in a while to prove that they uphold the law. Do you understand?" he asked. I nodded, not understanding any of it.

Neighbors watched the scene from behind their porch windows. Many felt a mixture of pity and relief; pity for their good neighbor and relief that the raid had not been on their home and still.

Within minutes my father appeared on our neighbor's front stoop. I ran out to him and rapidly began to relate the events, but he stopped me by saying, "I know, I know, I saw it all from across the street." I couldn't believe his words. My father had let the policeman take my mother to jail. I began to punch him with my fists.

"You let Mama go to jail. You hurt Mama like that. I hate you. I hate you!" I screamed.

My father let me have my hysterical moment, and as the shouts became sobs he held me close to him and tried to explain. He had seen the police van and car in our driveway. If he had come home, he would have been arrested, not only for housing the still but also for being the bootlegger. My mother would only be accused of having a still on the premises. My father could bail her out and eventually pay the fine.

"I could help Mama, but Mama could not have helped me," he reasoned.

It was logical, but I was not convinced. I still thought that my father had done the wrong thing, allowing the police to arrest my poor mother.

We went to the basement to inspect the damage. The policeman had used an ax on some parts of the still, but most of it was intact. All the filled bottles and cartons had been confiscated.

"It's not too bad," he said. "Now let's go and bring Mama home."

Bill drove us to the police station, stopping first to get a bail bondsman to put up the bail for Mama's release. A lawyer friend of the family told my father something he should do that would let him take my mother's place when the case came to trial.

Uncle Jerome was released first. He was held only as a witness. I was furious. Again, he acted as a boarder, sharing our food and home, but none of the troubles. My mother came out a back door of the station. I ran to her. She walked past my father as if he were not there.

All the way home she remained silent. When we arrived home, she went upstairs to her bedroom. My father started up after her, but was stopped when my mother called down, "Stay away. I don't want to hear you or see you." He saw her red eyes and angry face and knew that this was not the time to apologize. I heard the water running into the bathtub. My mother went into the bathroom, locked the door, and remained there for quite a while. Then she went to the bedroom and never came back downstairs that night.

My father made dinner for my brother and me. He refused to talk about what had happened. My brother went out to play stickball, seemingly unconcerned. My father picked up his newspaper and went to the sun parlor. The silence in the house was scary. I cried myself to sleep, worrying about my mother, confused about my father, and sorry for hating him as I did at that moment. I was ashamed to face my friends the following day. How could I explain the police car and van, and my mother going to jail?

The silence lasted for days. Finally, one evening at dinner, in a burst of anger my mother yelled, "I told you it would happen. The bums come and go out of this house. Jailbirds, thieves, *gonifs*, all of them. The murderer in the striped suit, he told the cops to get even with you. You bring crooks into your house. If you don't care about me, at least you should care about your children. You're as bad as those bums—you're no good, no good!"

Her tirade over, she exhaustedly fell into her kitchen chair and sobbed as if her heart was breaking. My father sat stiffly and said nothing. He pushed his chair away from the table and left the house. Hours later he returned home carrying a bunch of lilacs, my mother's favorite flowers. My mother took them in silence. She took a vase from the closet, put water in it, and arranged the lilacs to her liking. The silence continued. Looks, but no sound. Finally, my father spoke.

"What I did was wrong, but I had no choice. But I do have one choice. I have a choice of letting my family lose the roof over their heads, or making whiskey. I choose making whiskey. Next time, I'll go to jail, but my wife and family will eat and live here. I do care about you, but I care my way. I can't accept home relief and I can't beg, so I guess I'll just go on being a bootlegger."

He got up and left again. I stared at my mother. She almost smiled. I knew that I loved my father again. I think my mother did, too.

ENTER THE JUDGE

$\mathcal{A}$t this time, a new friend entered our lives. Judge Mueller. The trial was set for early June. My father's lawyer briefed him on what to plead. My father came home from a preliminary hearing at the Bronx County Courthouse. He seemed less frightened than the night before. He was buffered by the turn of events. He had pleaded guilty to having a still on the premises, but not to making whiskey for public consumption. A technicality! The judge summoned the arresting policemen to the bench to clarify the events of the day of the raid. My father's lawyer asked that the evidence, the alleged cases of whiskey, be produced in court. Confusion reigned in the courthouse. After further consultation among the judge, the lawyer, and the policeman, the hearing ended. My father was warned that the still would have to be de-

stroyed no matter who the owner was. My happy but puzzled
father thought that American justice was wonderful, but
strange. His lawyer cleared up the confusion. The policemen
had taken their share of the confiscated whiskey after they
had given the judge his due. No cartons of evidence, no case,
no trial!

Before he left the courtroom, the judge asked my father
to see him privately in his chambers. "Before you shut down
your business," the judge asked, "do you think that you
could deliver two cases of your very finest to the Westchester
Country Club? My daughter's wedding is in two weeks. Since
it's a family affair, it's not the same as a public party. We'll
keep it to ourselves. Who will know? Right?"

My father was delighted to be able to do the judge a favor—even if it was illegal. Only in America!

When he told my mother the story, she was hardly
pleased. "That makes the honorable judge a dirty crook,
too," she said, shaking her head in disbelief. "What a crazy
world! A crook is let go by a bigger crook. And I went to
jail—for what?" she yelled and began to cry.

She felt better when she met Judge Mueller when he visited us at our house one evening. He arrived in a big black
convertible touring car. All the kids on the street came to examine it. Judge Mueller was a handsome man, his iron gray
hair framing his ruddy, deep-lined face. My mother told us
that his twinkling blue eyes could not have been the eyes of
a *gonif.* He was very polite to my mother, commiserating with
her on her short stay in the police station. He even talked to

me about his three grandchildren, who were close to my age. Then he and my father went to the sun parlor and closed the French doors behind them. They transacted whatever business the judge had with my father, and the judge left in his car—after my father put a carton on the rear seat.

Judge Mueller became a steady visitor. His visits always ended with a carton or two being placed on the rear seat of his car.

One evening he came to the house and spent hours talking to my father. I awoke during the night hearing sounds of voices laughing and singing. The sounds were coming from the sun parlor. My father and the judge were quite drunk. Each time they said something, they would roar with laughter. I had never seen my father take a drink. His stomach could not tolerate alcohol. My father told me to go back to bed. He was going to take the judge home. The two of them staggered to their feet and left by the porch door, arm in arm, my father and his friend.

The next morning we found both my father and the judge asleep on the lounge chairs on the porch. When dad awoke, he looked terrible. His face was ashen, his eyes red-rimmed and clouded. He was holding his stomach and making strange moaning sounds.

The judge awoke and came into the kitchen. He smiled at my mother and asked, "What am I doing here? I thought I went home."

"You did," Dad answered. "I walked you home, but when I left you, you said you couldn't let me walk home alone. So you walked me back here." The judge laughed. My father laughed. Even my mother thought that it was funny and laughed with them.

The judge went to the bathroom to clean himself up, so as to look presentable for his return home. Before he left, he thanked my mother.

He said, "Albert, that whiskey of yours must be right off the boat. We were drinking the real McCoy last night."

My father nodded, but I knew that it had been made nowhere but in our basement. The judge left, but this time he left alone.

My mother said that she really liked him. "He's a real gentleman, not like the bums who come in and out of here," she added. She would not let my father think that her approval of the judge signified approval of Dad's way of life.

That evening my father became quite ill. He vomited several times. I heard my mother say that he vomited blood. I put the blanket over my head to shut out his moans and cries, and tried to sleep. By morning it was evident that my father had harmed himself by drinking. Dr. Weiss came and told my mother something that made her cry. She told it to my brother and me: Dad was very sick and had to be taken to the hospital, probably to stay for a long time.

Hospital rules prohibited children from visiting patients in the wards. I wrote to my father almost every day, drawing pictures at the bottom of the letters.

When he came home a few weeks later, Grandma Lubin came to stay with us to care for him. I think my father loved

her more than he cared for his own mother. The doctor prescribed a limited diet, mainly an enriched milk drink. He
warned my father that another upset like this one could cost
him his life. Each day Grandma would help my mother take
a wicker sun-parlor chair outside to the stoop. Wrapped in a
blanket, my father sat out there all afternoon, where the sun
would be good for him. He accepted his milk drink every few
hours, but grumbled about how hungry he was. Ignoring his
comment, Grandma and Mother went about their chores,
checking on him every few hours.

Gradually he put on a few pounds, his ashen look disappeared, and his spirits were better. One day, my uncle came
to visit him. When he got off the trolley he thought he saw
my father in the delicatessen that had just opened on Soundview Avenue. He couldn't believe it, but as he neared the
restaurant he did see my father eating the fattiest corned beef
sandwich imaginable. He screamed at my father and brought
him home. Everyone yelled, shouted, ranted, and raved at the
same time. Grandma went to our neighbor's house to use his
telephone to call Dr. Weiss. Dr. Weiss arrived within minutes,
expecting to see a dead man.

"Are you crazy?" he asked. "Don't you know that the food
could kill you? You can only drink Fermelac and eat potatoes
and rice. If you don't listen, you'll be dead in a month," he
warned.

He examined my father, mumbled and probed, prodded
and mumbled more.

"Hm, he seems to be all right. The diet is working. He's

even gained weight," he said, with a pleased-with-himself smug smile. "Now let me tell you—" he said, but my father interrupted him.

"No, let me tell you something. Every day for the past two weeks, when these women brought me the milk, I spilled it into the rosebushes. Then I went to the delicatessen and had a corned beef or pastrami sandwich with potato salad and a Dr. Brown's celery tonic. That's what cured me. If I drank only your fancy milk, I'd still be thin or dead. Incidentally, the milk didn't even help the rosebushes."

Everyone stared. Nobody spoke, then Dr. Weiss said, "Well, I gave you a warning, but ..." The doctor gave up his lecture.

My father looked at my grandma, winked, and said that he was ready for her great cooking.

"You're impossible." She laughed and went inside. She returned immediately, calling to my mother, "If he's well enough to eat, he's well enough to bring the chair in and get back to doing some work."

The next day she went home. My father never took a drink again.

Having the judge's protection gave my father a sense of security and a continued flow of some money to his pocket. I was not surprised when he decided to spend a good portion on a party for my tenth birthday instead of saving it for lean days ahead. My mother mumbled, "God forbid he can hold on to it. It's burning a hole in his pocket."

My cousins, neighborhood friends, my aunts, and of

course my grandma Lubin were invited, all bringing gifts. On the practical side I received woolen scarves, gloves, hair bows, a briefcase, and knee socks. But some gifts were for my entertainment—drawing paper pads, pastels, crayons, and colored paper. And books! I received several Nancy Drew volumes and three books written by my favorite author, Louisa May Alcott, *Little Women, Eight Cousins,* and *Rose in Bloom.* It couldn't be better.

The room was decorated with colorful streamers crossing and crisscrossing the ceiling. At the point where all the streamers met, a cluster of balloons was hung. At each table setting there was a birthday paper cup, paper plate, and party hat. Little tin watercolor paint sets, crayons, hand-held puzzles to test your skill, and jigsaw puzzles were placed at each setting as a favor for each child to take home. Each child entertained, reciting a poem, singing a song, or telling a joke. We played Blind Man's Bluff and Pin-the-Tail-on-the-Donkey, winners getting a prize.

Then the room was darkened. My mother came in carrying the most beautiful cake I ever saw. Roses and tulips and a ribbon of pink sugar outlined the message "Happy Tenth Birthday."

Ten candles, plus one more "to grow on," were ablaze. I was delighted and embarrassed at the same time. We gorged ourselves on cake, Dixie cups (half chocolate ice cream, half vanilla), cream soda, and our own boxes of animal crackers.

After everyone left, my father gave me my parents' gift to me. It was my first wristwatch. I was overcome with joy, hugging and kissing my mother and father. Then my grandma gave me her gift. It was her cameo, a lady carved out of coral set in an oval white gold frame. The lady had a thin chain with a diamond chip around her neck. It was the brooch I had seen on my grandma's clothes as long as I could remember. This was a true gift of love.

I told my mother that this was the best day of my whole life and I would remember it forever. My mother hugged me and, being a realist, she said, "I'm glad. Enjoy it." The wordless pause that followed seemed to say, "For as long as you can."

I was riding high on the top of the roller coaster. I didn't want to worry about tomorrow. Being surrounded by people who loved me so much was enough to make the reality of the Depression disappear—for at least a little while.

We never saw the judge again after my father's illness. My father never heard from him. They had an agreement that Dad would never call him or come to him. Dad said that the judge was probably embarrassed by his drunken behavior that night and didn't want to come back to our house.

A few months later, we heard that the judge was involved in some political scandal and resigned his seat in the court. It may have been just a coincidence, but shortly after his resignation our basement was raided again, and this time the still was completely smashed.

Perhaps it was also a coincidence that the irreparable damage was done when no member of the family was at home, and no summons was issued for my father's arrest as either the proprietor or the distiller.

The street buzzed with the story of the second raid on our house, the tale becoming more exaggerated with each telling, until our basement still became as infamous in the community as Al Capone's bootlegging empire.

Then just as the street was settling down to an unexciting, uneventful daily existence, a police van appeared in Mr. Wagner's driveway, blocking his hearse. Mr. Wagner, who was not too friendly a neighbor, now aroused the curiosity of the block; men emerged from doorways and stoops, maliciously pleased to see the van. Others gathered to see and hear why Mr. Wagner was being visited by New York's finest. Why were they entering the home of this self-proclaimed upstanding member of the community, one of the few who enjoyed steady employment—night and day—seven days a week?

Minutes passed. Mr. Wagner appeared with his usual dour expression, accompanied by three policemen. From his driveway he climbed the two steps into the rear of the van and sat on one side bench. One policeman entered the van and sat opposite him; the next went to the driver's seat. The third officer took the wheel of the hearse.

Both vehicles left the driveway and turned left on Rosedale Avenue, moving very slowly, as if they were part of a regular funeral cortege—except that the van preceded the hearse. The neighbors stared in puzzlement as the small procession drove slowly to the corner, turned left on Westchester Avenue and disappeared from sight.

Rumors of what might have happened to Mr. Wagner replaced the stories of my family's mishaps. Several days passed before Mr. Wagner returned—on foot, without his hearse. The always somber Mr. Wagner now seemed even more so; his cheerless expression was a mirror of his dejected feelings and his total indifference to his neighbors and their curiosity.

Perhaps it was the newly established bond—the bootlegger bond—between my father and Mr. Wagner that finally let him divulge the events that led up to his arrest and subsequent short jail sentence and fine. As he compared the two raids, the story unfolded. Mr. Wagner was an undertaker by day, but he used his hearse as a pickup and delivery service for a bootlegging network of small-time gangsters. By day he drove the deceased from home to funeral parlor to cemetery. At night he drove the hearse, with a coffin now loaded with bottles of bathtub gin and bootleg whiskey, from underground distilleries to speakeasies. By daytime his hearse was back in the driveway awaiting a call for its use as a funeral car. Until the day of the raid he had led this double life, enjoying the profits both made him. He thought he had done nothing wrong: nobody was hurt by his actions. My father agreed, and the two men shook their heads over the sad end of their businesses.

There were those who had believed Mr. Wagner was the informant for the neighborhood raids in the past. Now, the question arose once more—who was the person who had called the police to report the illegal stills? Were the aloof

Fairmont sisters the culprits? Or were the raids the consequences of the good judge's protection having ceased with
his own dishonor, thus opening a Pandora's box of question-
able relationships? The fear that our block was now targeted
for repeated police action brought bootlegging as a means of
making a living to an abrupt halt.

Mr. Wagner remained in his house and was rarely seen in
the street. His hearse, impounded by the police, never reap-
peared in his driveway. Suddenly, the man who was the subject of childish ridicule and mystery became just a pitiable
neighbor who had lost his livelihood, yet another unem-
ployed victim of the Depression.

The Fairmont sisters continued to peer past their white
lace curtains, contemptuous of their crooked neighbors,
happy that the legal system still worked in their behalf, daily
flying an American flag from the flagpole affixed to their
front porch. It didn't really matter whether or not they were
guilty of ratting on their neighbors. Their attitude and behavior bespoke guilt. Needing an answer, we decided the Fair-
monts were the informants, without proof or facts to confirm
their treachery. It was necessary to close the book on the
events—this was the end and we had to move on to other
topics, other problems, and find a way to face the stark days
ahead.

BEATING THE SYSTEM

*W*ith the destruction of our basement still, our household at last fully joined the ranks of the Great Depression's victims. Free vegetables that would otherwise have rotted in the ground or on the vines added to almost meatless meat loaf made up our standard, austere fare. Into a pound of ground meat my mother mixed in the usual stale bread, an egg or two, onions, potatoes, tomatoes, and any vegetables we were allowed to take from the farm—these with many spices made it possible to stretch the leftovers for several meals. Our Saturday visits to my grandmother with the leftovers she gave us made up the rest of our week's food supply.

My father joined the ranks of the vacant-eyed, blank-faced stoop-sitters for a short time. The number of men who sat and stared into space grew day by day. They were silent;

sharing their pain and shame was not allowed in their way of life. Men who formerly could boast of modest successes could not even talk of what they considered their failures. The first shock of the loss of their jobs or businesses gave way to anger and frustration and finally to despair and humiliation. Eager and anxious to work at any job that could earn them even a few pennies, they were unwilling to accept government handouts, and were afraid of the consequences of not enough food or shelter for their household. Shame was the name of the game.

Moving vans appeared on the block every day. Sometimes our neighbors left without even saying good-bye. Houses were foreclosed; some were boarded up. But my father could not accept this way of life. Early each morning he would leave for wherever it was he went each day. Each night he'd return empty handed. He was very quiet. He would read the many newspapers he retrieved from trash cans, eat what was put in front of him, and leave the house again. He and my mother rarely spoke to one another. One evening, I heard her say, "I guess even the bootlegging was better than this." My father slammed his hand on the table in anger, but said nothing.

When we had moved into our house in Clason Point, we had to buy additional furniture for the larger space. As did many families at the time, we had bought it on the installment plan, paying a fraction of the price of each item every month. We bought an oak dining-room set, a breakfront, wicker sun-parlor furniture, and an Oriental rug. One day, when I came home from school, I found the dining room empty. My father said that the furniture had been repossessed for nonpayment. That was only the beginning. Eventually we did without the breakfront, the Oriental rug, the armoire, and the wicker sun-parlor furniture, and ultimately our car was towed away.

The one thing that remained was the glass-enclosed bookshelves. My father bought several series of classics in red, blue, green, and brown leatherette, purchased one book at a time. Eventually we had the complete works of Shakespeare, Dickens, Mark Twain, Dumas, Hawthorne, and many more. *The Book of Knowledge*, a twelve-volume encyclopedia in its own bookcase, was purchased on time.

From my earliest memory, books were always an important part of my life. As a Jew, my father always quoted the age-old Jewish reason for having books and an education: "They can take your house, your land, your business, but they can never take what you have up here," he said, pointing to his head.

Before I learned to read, my mother sat me on her lap and read stories from Grimms' or Andersen's fairy tales. But my favorite book was an enormous, beautifully illustrated *Stories from the Bible*. Because it was so large, it was placed on the kitchen table and again I sat on my mother's lap as she turned the pages. She read me stories of Moses found in the bulrushes, Noah and the ark, Daniel in the lion's den, and many others.

My father let me know that he believed these to be stories not unlike the other fairy tales.

My mother frowned at him and asked, "Was that necessary?"

My father answered, "That's my opinion. Can't I tell her how I feel about these stories?"

To me he said, "Just enjoy the stories now. When you're a big person you'll decide if they're true stories or not. Okay?"

"Okay," I said quickly to end the discussion so my mother could continue to read to me and finish the stories. My father was not the father I knew. This man was a totally defeated person who moved through life as if it were a bad dream.

Books and Victrola records provided years of entertainment in our house. They were our defense against day after day of monotony when money was scarce or nonexistent and only your home and family could provide any degree of enjoyment.

The kitchen set was moved into the dining room, and odds and ends of additional furniture were borrowed from relatives. Luckily, the Stromberg-Carlson radio had been paid for completely and was not repossessed with the other furniture. As unemployment grew those who were lucky enough to have a roof over their heads—and owned a radio—were the ones who had a source of entertainment. And it was free.

Programs were added to the Blue and Red network. Lowell Thomas delivered the bleak news. Father Coughlin, a priest who used radio as his pulpit, supposedly preached hope, but in fact he had a political agenda and became a spokesman for anti-Semitism. CBS finally forced him off the air.

With the theme song of "My Time Is Your Time," Rudy Vallee introduced many comedians to his audience. His variety program featured the talents of Jack Benny, Ed Wynn, Fred Allen, and others. Since vaudeville was on a downslide, these comedians found radio to be their new theater and soon all of them had their own variety programs. From Eddie Cantor to George Burns and Gracie Allen, we could count on many laughs.

Half-hour series were eagerly awaited from week to week. I laughed at the antics of Amos and Andy, smiled at Mollie Goldberg in her Bronx apartment calling to her friends from her window, and cried through the tribulations of "One Man's Family." Bing Crosby crooned and the Mormon Tabernacle Choir uplifted our spirits. Radio challenged our imaginations and filled our days and nights.

All through the earlier days of the Depression I had been aware that we were not exactly able to survive without Grandma Lubin's help. But now I knew how little we really had. As the food became less and less varied, as my shoes let water into my socks, as my sweaters were patched at the elbows, I realized that we were really poor. I saw the pain in my mother's eyes and the deep shame in my father's face. As a provider he had failed us, and his sense of disgrace affected his posture for months to come.

Finally our house was taken from us. It was foreclosed by the United States Bank, which held our small mortgage. My father had no means of keeping up the payments each month. For several months we received notices from the bank. Too proud, neither my mother nor my father would ask their families for help. Then we received warning notices of a possible dispossession. A notice from the city marshal was hand delivered to my mother stating that ten days hence was the actual day of eviction. On a cold, drizzly afternoon, I turned the corner of our block and saw our remaining furniture piled outside our house. My mother was sitting on a straight-backed wood kitchen chair, surrounded by hurriedly packed cartons of books, records, pictures—all our worldly possessions. Clothes were stacked on the sofa, with newspapers to protect them from the rain. The rest of the furniture was arranged in a high pile around her. One or two neighbors stood by to keep my mother company. They knew that they could be facing the same situation at any time. The marshal told my mother that the truck would take our furniture to a city warehouse. The city would hold it for a short while and then dispose of it if it was not claimed. He didn't mention where we would find shelter—that was not his job.

My mother was silent, her eyes red from crying. My father was nowhere to be seen. I buried my head on my mother's shoulder and cried with her. I didn't want to stay with any of our relatives. I knew that we would probably have to stay with someone on my father's side of the family. My mother would never let her own family know how desperate our situation was. She did not want to hear her brothers' criticism of my father or their constant refrain of "I told you so, I told you not to marry him." My mother and I would have a roof, albeit an unpleasant one, over our heads, I thought. My brother wouldn't join us. He would stay with a friend. Would my father come with us? The family was being split up. We were falling apart.

Suddenly the specter of Hooverville was before me. Would my father live among those homeless men without families whom I had seen that day when we walked home from Westchester Avenue? Would my father be alone like that grizzly bearded one who offered me a potato? Suddenly the man who had given me that little carved deer was just a poor guy—not unlike my father—who had probably lost everything and was unable to keep his family together. Would my father become like that isolated man, who appeared to be so old and ragged? Would my family ever be together again? In my mind the Depression stood for the destruction of a family. That was the crux of it. Now the Depression had really come to my family—and it was literally tearing us apart. I held on to my mother and sobbed.

From nowhere my father appeared. He walked over and spoke to the city marshal.

"I know it's not your fault. You're just doing your job," he said, apologizing *for* the marshal. He pointed across the street to another house. The marshal nodded, slapped my father on the shoulder as if he were an old friend. They shook hands. My mother and I were bewildered. What scheme was my father involved in with the marshal?

My father said, "Come with me. We're moving into our new home across the street."

He took my hand; I took my mother's hand.

He took the keys from his coat pocket and opened the front door of a red-brick house diagonally opposite our old home. When the truck came, the marshal instructed the men to move our belongings to our new home.

Suddenly my father was the man I had always known. He smiled, he chatted, he was friendly—and he had a new dream.

Within an hour my mother had the floors swept and was busily engaged in washing the windows. She dug the white sheer curtains out of the carton, found the brass rods and put them over the windows.

"Curtains make a house a home," she said. She stepped back to admire her work.

"Now it looks lived in," she said happily.

At once she was cheerful, forgetting the day's events. She barked orders at my brother and me. The dishes were unpacked, washed, and put in the kitchen closets. Clothes were hung up. Beds were made.

Neighbors came to see our new home and wondered how we were so fortunate as to get relocated so quickly. I wondered too, but I believed in miracles again. My father was himself again. He had performed his magic, transforming a tragedy into a triumph over the evil Depression.

While we were doing our chores, my father went to find Nick, his friend and jack-of-all-trades. Nick came back to our house and gave us the use of the gas and electricity—being adept at breaking the Bronx Gas and Electric Company's special locks. This was Nick's secret weapon against big business. We were back in the bootlegging business, but this time we were bootlegging the services of the utility company.

I had no idea how my father was able to pull off this miracle of a new home. I didn't discover the answer for several months. He knew from the first that it would be just a matter of weeks before the city marshal actually evicted us. But he took a gamble on the times in which we lived and his knowledge of human nature. He went to the bank which held the mortgages on the houses on the other side of the street. For that interview, he put on his best suit, the only one that was not shiny with age and wear. (His other suits had found their way to the high-cash clothes man who took turns with street performers making a living in the alleys of our neighborhood.) He didn't look exactly prosperous, but he didn't look poor either. Dad told a minor bank employee that he was looking for a house for his family, and he knew of several houses that were foreclosed and unoccupied on Rosedale Avenue in Clason Point. The banker was more than pleased with Dad's interests. There were many vacant ones he would love to sell or even rent, and here was a possible buyer.

Since the bank, like all other businesses, was operating

with a skeleton staff, they offered my father the keys to several houses. My father had already decided on 754, and politely thanked his benefactor-to-be. An hour later he had a duplicate key made and returned all to the bank. He said that he would think about the houses and let the bank know his decision as soon as possible. Dad returned the original set of keys, pocketing the duplicate key to number 754. They shook hands. A few days later, with the city marshal's help, my father moved his family from the sidewalk to our new home across the street.

With a new but similar roof over our heads, electricity and gas in operation, and a little food in our stomachs, my father rejoiced in having taken still another step toward "beating the system." I was happy to have my good old father back with us.

In time, we had new dining-room furniture, a breakfront, and a new Oriental rug, all bought on time. When my mother questioned my father about these purchases, he'd answer, "Don't worry. There's no still in the basement." My mother said little but worried a great deal. I wondered where the money was coming from, but I guessed that my father knew what he was doing.

The bubble suddenly burst. Whatever my father had been doing to get a little money ended abruptly. No more came into the house. My father still left early each morning, coming back empty handed and dejected each evening. Where he went or what he did every day, I never knew. Once in a while he came home with a bag of apples or a chicken, but we never knew where he got them. He read endlessly, but seemed to find no pleasure in it. Once again much of our furniture was repossessed. The rooms stood empty.

One afternoon, he came home from my uncle's paint store with cans of paint. When Mama and I went on our weekly Saturday visit to Grandma's house, my father pulled himself out of the doldrums by painting my bedroom. Unfortunately, my uncle had given my father gallons of unsalable colors. We came home that evening to find the walls of my room painted light blue, the molding and trim silver, and the ceiling dark blue with silver stars dotting the sky. My mother was furious. I didn't know what to make of it. My father was disappointed by our reactions. My friends thought that it was swell. I began to like it. On subsequent Saturdays he surprised us with a stippled textured dinette, an all-silver bathroom, and a sponge-painted staircase wall. We learned to live with all these colors and textures. But these diversions were not enough for my father, a man who rarely admitted defeat, but was indeed being defeated by the times.

We did, however, manage to keep one step ahead of our local utility company. Every time Bronx Gas and Electric Company disconnected our services by putting a lock on our kitchen meter, Nick would come over to break the lock with his special tool. This became a monthly activity. Whenever our service was curtailed, I learned to read and do my homework by candlelight. One evening I fell asleep at the dining table and was awakened suddenly by the smell of singed hair. I had burned my bangs and singed one eyebrow in the burning candle. Nick was called to break the lock on the meter.

Consolidated Bronx Gas and Electric Company took a more drastic step. The utility line under the street bringing service to our house was finally closed off. Late one night, Nick arrived with a new device. It was a strange-looking wrench attached to a long broomstick. With a flashlight as his light source, he went to do battle with his personal windmill—the utility company. He removed the steel plate that covered the pipeline. He lowered his special wrench into the hole. The stick went down until only the top of it was partly visible, and then he rotated it until he heard a click. He had done it, he had broken the main lock.

"Let there be light," my father called, and there was light! "We did it again, Nick," my father said, slapping him on the back.

But Nick did not respond at first. I never saw him so quiet. When he began to speak, he spoke in anger.

"Did you see what they did to us in Washington? We were peaceful. We only wanted what was comin' to us. Some soldiers were in tents with their wives and kids, too. What harm could they do? We were promised a bonus and now we need it. I get a little money for losin' my leg for this lousy country, but a lot of those guys get nuttin' and their family is starvin'."

The words tumbled out. His face was red and a vein stood out on his forehead. My father touched his arm, but he wanted no sympathy, no appeasement. He continued, his raspy voice showing his anger and pain.

"The bastard—excuse me—Hoover told the soldiers to drive us out. We are soldiers who went to war for this country. We wasn't beggin'. We were askin' for *our* money. The cavalry charged into us, knockin' us down. That fart—excuse me—General MacArthur had the army chase us out of Washington." He started to cry. "For this lousy country, I lost a leg."

He sobbed unashamedly. My father and I cried with him. My mother heard a little of it, but knew enough to feel that Nick was treated badly by the government.

The next day we read all about the terrible disaster of the "Bonus March," but most newspapers, my father noted, "sided with the president." The World War I veterans had met in Washington to demonstrate their need for government assistance—assistance which they thought was their due. They had been promised a bonus for their participation in the army and navy during the war. The veterans camped out on the lawns and deserted buildings in Washington, D.C., some with families, and were accused of a variety of civil and criminal activities. The newspapers damned the bonus marchers for being tools of communist organizations and not being veterans at all. President Hoover told General MacArthur to disband the group. General MacArthur turned the cavalry loose to rout these poor veterans, and they did so with sabers drawn and horses at full gallop, trampling tents and their occupants without regard for the women and children inside them. They threw torches made of rolled paper into the tent city, setting the area into a blaze that could be seen from all parts of the capital. It was a national crime—a crime perpetrated by a callous president who could close his eyes and mind to the desperation of the people, and whose claim to fame was to have shantytowns named for him.

Nick told us more about himself that night than in all the years we had known him. He was not alone. My uncle Ben had been with the American Expeditionary Force in France, and he was outraged by the news. Unlike Nick he was not an activist and did not go to Washington, but he found it difficult to understand how one U.S. soldier could fire on another, a veteran who had probably fought right by his side in 1917. But my uncle dismissed it all with a wave of his hand and his usual expression: "You can't fight City Hall."

Nick was deeply scarred and disillusioned about his country, but was the better man for it. He did something to help himself and his buddies instead of just complaining about it.

I read the news articles vindicating President Hoover. Editorials pressed the point that many of the men were Bolsheviks plotting to overthrow the government. I didn't know what a Bolshevik was, but I was sure that simple, loyal, unpolitical Nick was not one of them. I wondered how the country could turn against the veterans who had fought and honored their homeland just a few years before they were routed from Washington. Again, I was forced to examine what I had always taken for granted—this time my patriotism, my belief in my country right or wrong. I wondered if even my country could make a mistake.

My father's enthusiasm for his new country began to wane. The Bonus March stuck in his mind. Doubts were creeping into his thoughts about the causes of the Depression, the inequities in the different classes of American society.

My grandfather Kellerman always thought of himself as a successful businessman. Coming from a wealthy European family, he saw the Republican party as the one which spoke for his ideas and ideals. My father, always in business for himself, always an entrepreneur, also allied himself at the polls with the Republican party. When I was old enough to become aware of the goals of the Democrats and Republicans, I questioned my father's choice. He shared his home with anyone who had none and would give away his last penny or piece of bread. My father was a registered Republican, thought like a Democrat and acted like a socialist. He was an enigma. The more I learned about him, the more complicated he became. When I lay awake sorting out all my thoughts, I began to understand that one person could be many people, the personality changing with each relationship. But to me he was simply my father, and I was his pride and joy.

Life in Clason Point continued on a downward spiral. Bread lines and soup kitchens sprang up in stores and churches. Survival became more difficult with each passing day. Our survival became more dependent upon my grandmother's food packages each weekend.

When we visited my aunt who lived in a cold-water flat on

Ninth Avenue, we walked along the Hudson River. More and more people were living in makeshift hovels along the river, and shantytowns were even springing up in Central Park.

On Rosedale Avenue there was more stoop sitting than ever before. More boarded up houses. More good-byes. More tears. The streets became a communications network. "Did you hear Mrs. Amasano's sister died?" a neighbor asked. She knew because Mrs. Amasano was called to a telephone in another neighbor's house, the only one who still had a phone. The call was usually a prelude to news of some family tragedy. The neighbors would not abuse the telephone, using it only if it was an emergency.

Other less personal news was delivered by a newsboy shouting, "Extra! Extra!" if the news was really newsworthy. So it was in March of 1933 that we learned of the Lindbergh child's kidnapping. Ignoring the fact that the child was kidnapped for ransom from a well-known, wealthy family, my mother and our neighbors became fearful and overprotective of their own children and kept a constant watch over protesting boys and girls. Curfews were set by our parents. Boundaries for playing were drawn back to a few square blocks. We lived with the kidnapping news on a daily basis, and when the child was found dead a kind of mourning pall was cast over the neighborhood.

People with few or no financial resources felt pity for the Lindberghs, whose wealth could not spare them from tragedy. Mr. Ferrara said that this was a funny twist—to his knowledge it was the first time that money was the cause of a tragedy. Neighbors shook their heads in agreement. Looking upward he called on God and asked, "Why? Y'took my Giuseppe an' we had nuttin'. Now y'took a little bambino who had everytin'. It isn't right. So why?"

Mrs. Ferrara felt personally sorry for Mrs. Lindbergh. "A mother know how she musta feel. A mother know," she repeated. But with a deep sigh she added, "It's God's will. He knows why." Her husband shook his head sadly. The women who had the luxury of believing agreed that there was a reason for everything. The men seemed to be bitter and angry at the turn of events that destroyed their ability to earn a living and provide for their families, thus taking away their manhood. They saw no solace in God's will.

My father rarely went to the synagogue. He thought that religious feeling did not depend on a building, a priest or a rabbi. But our Catholic neighbors had always attended church on Sundays, both mother and father, with children in tow—the complete family. It seemed to me as the Depression continued that only the women went to church, with protesting children following behind. Were the times taking their spiritual toll as well? Or was it just the end of hope in any form? Everything was changing with the times.

Many vacant houses were used for a night's shelter by the drifters who passed through Clason Point searching for a day's work on the farms, or at least some free vegetables, theirs for just the picking. Hoovervilles grew in size and number on all the vacant lots in Clason Point. Now entire families inhabited the makeshift homes. Inventive people made homes out of huge cartons, corrugated tin sheets, and discarded lumber from aborted housing starts, and they used felled trees as posts, to hold up multicolored, many-patterned, worn-out carpets as walls and roofs. Large steel drums were fired up for warmth and cooking and usually became the center of a group of men talking about their fears for any kind of future. Hope was gone. Tomorrow was a nightmare of more pain to come. Dignity was lost. Poverty was the way of life.

Their children looked like miniature editions of the desperate adults. Their eyes had the same dull, dead look; rarely was laughter heard in these encampments. The children were growing up and growing old before their time. Even the young women appeared much older than their chronological age. Their weather-beaten skin looked like leatherette, and they too had the vacant stare of hopelessness. My father, haunted by these scenes, spoke to my mother of our good fortune in having a roof over our heads. My mother only muttered, "Amen," before she sadly shook her head and added, "But for how long?"

All through my childhood I heard my mother's pessimistic comments, her constant refrain: "But what will tomorrow bring?" My father's optimism was unrealistic; she believed in seeing things as they really were—not through the rosy glasses she accused my father of wearing. So my life teetered between my parent's view of half-full or half-empty glasses, sometimes worrying as my mother did, and full of my dad's dreams at other times.

To alleviate the hopeless situation and to raise the spirits of the occupants of Hooverville, twice a month a city truck pulled into a vacant lot on Soundview Avenue. A large white screen, covering the side of the truck, was unfurled, loud-speakers were strategically placed in tree, branches, and a movie projector was anchored to a tree stump. A feature film, cartoons, and a sing-along short of the follow-the-bouncing-ball type encouraging the audience to join in a community sing as the lyrics flashed on the screen were shown. Despite the times, the site of the theater, and the bare ground as seats, the audience sang along with gusto.

For a while, the ragged audience was drawn into the world as seen through the lens of the Hollywood camera— the world of wise-cracking Joan Blondell and a chorus of high-kicking dancers, of Ruby Keeler, the understudy who becomes a star, of the leading man Dick Powell who always made good, and all the boy-meets-girl stories with their in-evitable happy endings. The audience was lifted from their own lives in an ugly environment into a magic world of make-believe, changing reality into fantasy, tears into laugh-ter, and hopelessness into wishful dreams. The movie ended, the screen was rolled up, the speakers and projector re-moved—the magic was gone and people drifted back to their own vacant lots, to their own hovels, to the real world; but for a few hours, the movie became the topic of conversation, and smiles lit up their usually sad faces. Another week or so would bring another truck, another movie, another escape into the world of dreams.

As we walked home from the movie, I realized how lucky we were to be going home to a real house with four walls, ceilings, real floors and windows and doors. Did the movie world really exist? Was this what drove my father—this elusive dream that he could achieve success that was possible only in America? How often I heard him use that phrase to explain to my mother that one day our trying time would end, that there really was a pot of gold at the end of the rainbow. My mother answered that first you had to find the rainbow, and she didn't see one in the foreseeable future.

I was surprised when a neighbor criticized the free movie, suggesting that movies caused more grief than good. He remarked that the homeless became angry and agitated by the lavish lifestyles portrayed in them. He said, "How could these people living in squalor watch the movie without resentment? It will only fuel the fire of discontent. Wait and see." My father told me not to worry, that Mr. Lambert was an ex-union organizer and was considered a radical thinker by many of our neighbors. "Pay no attention to him. Enjoy the movies. Everybody does. There's time enough for trouble," he said.

The size of the audience grew with each performance, and the enthusiastic clapping after each show belied the fact that it caused viewers any grief. Mr. Lambert had to be wrong.

SCHOOL DAYS

*E*lementary school education was divided into two terms per school year, one commencing in September, the other in February. You spent half the year in an A class, the other in a B class, and you were promoted or left behind at the end of each half-year term. Without taking into consideration a child's social or emotional age, bright pupils were often skipped half a grade. I was skipped three times in elementary school, advancing me a year and a half beyond my neighborhood friends. I was doing mathematical problems and reading books at a different level, leaving behind the Bobbsey twins series. My chronologically older classmates were maturing physically and leaving me behind, and I was excluded from their secret intimate discussions. Being too old mentally for one group and too young socially for the other caused

144

many a teary afternoon as I speculated when, if ever, I would fit into a group of my peers. The problem was solved for me when I completed the sixth grade.

At the end of sixth grade, four of us were chosen to leave our eight-grade school to attend the rapid advancement classes at the Herman Ridder Junior High School. We were A students at the top of our grade. Coincidentally, three of us, Clara, Harold, and I, were the only Jewish children in the class. Genevieve was from a Dutch Protestant family. I was both excited and afraid of the change in school and education.

The Rapid Advancement classes completed three years of work in two years. R.A. covered seventh-grade work in six months' time, followed by six months of R.B. to complete the eighth-grade curriculum. R.C. and R.D. were actually the first year of high school, so before I was twelve years old I was to be in high school.

Since this move necessitated a lengthy trolley trip costing ten cents a day, our parents' permission was required. Fifty cents a week fed all of us at least one meal, but my father was very proud that I was chosen and decided to let me go. I had no idea where the fifty cents came from, but I accepted it. Each morning I joined my three friends to take the long trolley ride, involving two transfers, to arrive at our beautiful new art-deco design school.

The building fronted on Boston Road, and its rear exits faced Crotona Park East. After Clason Point, Boston Road and Southern Boulevard were for me the hub of the big city.

There were stores of every kind, restaurants, a library, and even movie houses. An elevated train roared overhead. The apartment buildings were six or eight stories high, and many had landscaped courtyards. People were everywhere. Crotona Park East was a beautiful street facing a park with huge trees and wide paths. I was in Wonderland.

I had neighborhood friends who were my age of eleven, but they were two years behind me in school. In eighth grade at Herman Ridder Junior High School my school reading list included the *Iliad* and the *Odyssey*, while they were still reading the Nancy Drew series. Some friends, like Edith, thought I was showing off.

At Herman Ridder, some of my classmates were two years older than I was. The girls whispered about the "curse" which they had every month. I vaguely knew that it was something that happened to older girls. The secret was kept to a small group in the know. I was a social misfit.

When I asked my mother to shed a little light on the subject, she seemed embarrassed, and her answer was vague and unsatisfactory. "You will get it when it's your time. You're not even eleven years old yet. You'll see." And she ended all further discussion.

If the "curse" was what I had to look forward to, I wasn't so sure that I wanted it.

In time, I found out what it was. On one of our Saturday visits a while later, when I was eleven years old, my mother whispered to my grandmother, "She just became a woman," and pointed to me.

My grandmother called me over to her. She smiled, hugged me, and then slapped me in the face. Tears welled up in my eyes. What had I done? But before I could ask, Grandma said, "Don't cry. That was a love tap. In Poland when a little girl becomes a woman her mama or grandma gives her a slap. That slap means that it should be the worst pain you should have for the rest of your life. You understand?"

I knew there had to be a good reason. My grandma would never hurt me.

The best part of getting the "curse" was that I finally fit in with at least one group in my junior high school.

Again there was a compulsory dress code (which was similar to my elementary school's) for Herman Ridder which made all of us—rich or poor—seem the same. This was another thing that helped me fit in with my peers.

Every evening I would bubble over with new excitement about the area and the school. It was a "progressive" school using Edward Maguire's "group study plan."

Many of my teachers were not happy with this progressive method of education. A class was divided into four groups. Each group was given a phase of the topic to discuss, take notes, and report its findings to the entire class. We met in the four corners of the room. There was always some student in the group who took the assignment seriously enough to get us to bring back some information to the class. The rest of us played word games or "Actors and Actresses" or just talked to use up the fifteen minutes of our group discussion.

Some of my teachers who were opposed to the plan (feeling we were not mature enough for independent study) set up a "chickie" system. It worked this way. The teacher followed the curriculum for the grade by teaching the class for the entire forty-five minute period. Each classroom had a front and a back door, the doors having windows in the upper half. One student's desk and chair was placed on guard at each door. When Dr. Maguire and the ever-present education guests were seen approaching the classroom, the student yelled "chickie" and we quickly went to the corners of the room in groups. The guests went from group to group, asked questions, took notes and left. Dr. Maguire thanked us and the teacher for the wonderful demonstration and said, "Keep up the good work."

Our teacher waited for a student at the door to say "All clear" and said, "Now let me go back to teaching and you get back to learning," and she smiled, acknowledging our part in the conspiracy.

Though the plan might have worked on paper, it was a disaster in practice. But we had a fine art teacher (who taught without the group method), and an English teacher who brought theater to the school. We had a magnificent auditorium and a small theater in the tower. Each class had to put on a play, and since we were supposedly gifted, our teacher thought that we should write one. The girls won out and decided to adapt Louisa May Alcott's *Little Women*. We chose the scenes and wrote the dialogue.

The highlight of my first term was this play—this moment in the sun. When it came time to cast the play, my physical appearance again came to my rescue. I looked like a frail Beth. I was short, very thin, and pale. Big brown eyes dominated my bony face, and I looked like I was at death's door, as if a light wind could easily blow me away. I was terrified. Stage fright took over, and consequently my last words were barely audible and thus even more convincing. The audience applauded when I died in Marmee's arms and the curtain fell. That night I told my family that I was going to be an actress or a writer, or maybe both.

I raved about my friend Regina Resnick, who played Marmee and sang solos at Friday assemblies. (Later she would become a star at the Metropolitan Opera.) I talked about my friend Marian Wolff, whose mother was a real schoolteacher. I couldn't imagine what it would be like to have an honest-to-goodness teacher for a mother.

My art teacher told my parents I showed promise. I joined the art club and fell in love with still another field of interest. I guessed that if my uncle Sam could write songs, my great-uncle Wolff could write newspaper articles, and my father's family could paint, there might be a chance for me. Anyway, I could dream. Being my father's daughter, I had dreams larger than life.

My parents listened to all my stories. My brother was

bored. He was a junior at James Monroe High School, and I was a junior high school brat. What a contrast to my previous four-room schoolhouse: I was in a block-long, four-storied building with a tower, central heating, two gymnasiums and a huge auditorium. I was happy despite the endless trolley trip. My family was convinced they had made the right decision allowing me to attend Herman Ridder Junior High School.

The days of the week were completely taken up with schoolwork, starting and ending each day with the long trip to and from school. My school day began at seven when I boarded the trolley and lasted until five when I finally reached home again. Homework kept me busy until nine. Saturdays I visited my grandma. Sunday was my day, and I often spent it at the movies.

In this school I was introduced to a great cross section of cultures, including children who came from Jewish backgrounds—quite a change from just four Jewish children in my entire elementary school. At the movies, I had felt detached from the Fox Movietone News when I saw events unfolding in Germany. Then I became friends with two Jewish girls who were in my German class. They were recent immigrants from Austria. Because I spoke a little German I was assigned to be their "buddy." In broken English and some German they told me why their parents left Munich and then Vienna.

Pauline said, "Our papa, he lose his work. No Jews work here anymore. Some friends not talk with us anymore. Why? Because we Jewish."

Ilsa added, "We leave Munich. We leave relatives and furniture and lots of coats and dresses. We go to Vienna. My papa think Vienna will be better."

They told me that Vienna was not better. Their father could not get a job as a bookkeeper and could only get menial jobs. When a boss discovered he was Jewish, he was fired again. They made friends only with other Jews and the parents worried about what would happen to their little girls.

Their stories frightened me. Could being a Jew be dangerous for me and my family? Didn't my grandma tell me stories about the terrible times Jews had in Poland when she was a little girl? But there was no feeling against the Jews in our neighborhood, even though most of the families were Italian Catholics. They didn't seem to care what their neighbors were as long as they were kind and friendly. They only worried about making a living.

When I mentioned my thoughts to Ilsa she said, "Ya, I us to tink same. We tink all are good. But they say, 'No, Jews no good. Get out!' So we go to Vienna. But even Vienna say Jews no good! So we go to America. Tings are better. But times change—who knows?" Ilsa was just my age, but she seemed so much older.

Pauline added, "Not to worry. America better. I not afraid here."

I remembered stories that my grandma used to tell me about her early life in Poland. These girls were like my grandma, leaving their home in Europe because they were

Jewish. It was hard for me to understand why being Jewish was a reason to be hated. Didn't Jewish families and Italian families get along with each other on Rosedale Avenue?

It was the first time I became aware of what anti-Semitism really meant and what it could do to a family or a whole community. Suddenly the radio and film news took on a new meaning. Germany was not just a faraway country with anti-Semitic policies; it was a country that persecuted my classmates Ilsa and Pauline.

I mentioned them to my father. He shook his head with impatience. "Where did you think all the greenies came from? Didn't you ever think why they came here?"

I said, "I never gave it much thought."

"Well, now you know why. You met two girls and *now* you question it. Do you know how many little girls and their families left their homes to come here? Here is better than there, even if it's not so good right now."

"Why doesn't someone help them?" I asked.

He sighed. "Many people do, but they need more than just people to help. A long time ago anti-Semitism forced us to come to America, but now it's much more in the open. You're just a child. All you can do is be nice to those little girls. They can learn from you, but you can learn a lot from them, too."

I was amazed that my father knew so much about the situation in Germany, but his concern for people touched me more. My father believed in people. Even though my mother continued to call him a patsy, my father still shared what little we had with others.

Late one afternoon, I was startled by the sight of an extremely tall black man standing on our front porch. He was dressed all in white from his turbaned head to his billowing pants. His white teeth shone in his shiny coal-black face. His appearance was menacing to me. He and my father were engaged in a quiet discussion as I reached the porch.

"This is my little girl," my father said.

The tall man took my hand in his massive one and held it gently. "Your father tells me you are in junior high school," he said in perfect English. "He is very proud of you, as I am of my children."

I mumbled, "Thank you," and withdrew my hand. Who was this man? Where did my father meet him? Why did he bring him home? All these questions ran through my head.

I heard my father say, "My friend is an Ethiopian Jew." And before I could speak, he anticipated my question. "Yes, he's a Jew. A black Jew. One of the lost tribes."

This was too much for me to comprehend. Not only did I not know where Ethiopia was but I didn't believe that a black man could be Jewish. How did my father know about Ethiopian Jews and lost tribes? What was this man doing in our house? Was he going to stay? What did my mother think?

My father answered one unspoken question. "He is here to raise money to help his starving people. I met him on

Westchester Avenue near the Elder Avenue Synagogue and I asked him to dinner."

I just nodded and I said I had homework to do. I was anxious to talk to my mother to get her reaction to my father's visitor. Her remarks surprised me. "Your father's at it again. He brings home a man to dinner without asking if we have enough or what we have. You don't feed company what you eat every day."

I was astonished that she didn't comment on the man's color. That did not seem to matter. What mattered to her was the lack of suitable food for a guest.

She continued. "And God knows what your father promised him. If the man is looking for money, he's come to the wrong house. You can't get blood from a turnip."

I asked, "Do you know he's Jewish?"

"So your father says," she replied. "The Bible mentions lost tribes and maybe theirs was a black tribe. But leave it to your father to find someone who's lost and bring him home. I hope he doesn't ask him to stay here. Dinner is enough. This is not a boarding house!"

I found my mother to be much more accepting of my father's newest friend than I had expected. If my mother welcomed him, I guessed I could too. But I could not believe that I was going to eat dinner with a colored man as our guest.

We sat down to dinner with my mother's stretched meal of watered-down soup, bread-extended meat loaf with hard-boiled eggs, leftover vegetables from the local farm, and fruit compote and tea. Somehow my mother had managed to pull off a meal when her pride was involved. The table was set with her special damask tablecloth, cloth napkins, the remaining pieces of Rosenthal china, and sparkling crystal stemware. As I peered over the brass candlesticks with the lit candles, I could see that our guest was pleased and impressed. Despite all her previous grumbling, my mother, too, was pleased with the evening. My father and his new friend sat on the porch talking far into the night.

We never saw him again, but we received postcards from various parts of the country as he traveled in an attempt to raise money and awareness of the plight of the Ethiopian Jews.

A few months after I started in my new school, our family's trials grew even worse. We had exhausted our coal supply and now burned twigs, wood crates, broken furniture, and finally our basement banister, in the furnace. The Bronx Gas and Electric Company, frustrated by my father in their attempt to deprive us of service, went to court, naming the U.S. bank as co-owner of the house. When the utility company cited my father for destruction of *their* property in the street fronting our house, my father countered with the illegality of their placing meters on *our* property. The bank was bewildered. Their records showed 754 Rosedale Avenue as a vacant house. An employee was sent to investigate the situation and, to his amazement, found our family living there. They started court proceedings to evict us. A first notice was sent out.

EXODUS

$\mathcal{M}$y father asked me how I would like to live closer to my new school. I had mixed feelings. I loved our house and neighbors, but I would not miss the long trip each day. "It's up to you," I said.

While I was doing my homework, I heard my parents discuss the possible move. The next morning my father accompanied me to school to look around the neighborhood and find us an apartment in the area. That night he told us of his find, a third-floor walk-up on East 174th Street.

"A big eat-in kitchen, two nice bedrooms, and a large living room," he reported. "The landlord will give us two months' concession and a new paint job. Oh yeah, I forgot. We get new shades, a new shower curtain, and a new toilet seat."

156

This was standard procedure for a new lease during the Depression. With the payment of one month's rent, we would be secure for three months. I gave little thought to where my father had gotten the money to pay even the first month's rent. I thought that my parents were happy, but my brother told me that it was a step down to move to an apartment, and we would again have to share a room. He was not pleased.

My parents wrapped our dishes in newspaper. My mother took down the curtains, folding them to use as cushions between the layers of breakable items in the cartons and barrels. The night before we moved, I overheard my mother tell my father at least one person would benefit from the move. I went into the kitchen to protest. I was not eager to be the cause of our need to move.

"Don't move on my account. I don't mind the trip," I told them.

My mother sat me on her lap and told my father to tell me the truth. He didn't look at me, but without raising his head he said, "We have to move. We got an eviction notice. We have to be out by Monday." He left the kitchen and walked out of the house. He was gone for hours, unable to face our troubled faces.

As the door shut behind my father, I sat at the kitchen table watching my mother carefully packing the last of the bric-a-brac. My thoughts focused on the different manner in which my parents faced their lives.

My father, hating controversy, usually walked away from painful conversations or situations. At his request, "Don't tell

Mama," I never confided troublesome secrets to my mother. But I suddenly realized that, although it was my father, the eternal optimist, who always felt that everything would finally work out and provided the excitement, the future plans, it was my mother who saw things the way they actually were and took care of our day-to-day existence, managing to feed us, clothe us, and keep an orderly home around us to the best of her ability, with the help of my grandmother.

I was not keeping bad news from my mother. She was well aware of our family situation. It was my mother who was protecting me from being hurt when my unfulfilled dreams died. She didn't want to destroy my hopes; she just wanted me to realistically see the possibilities.

My mother faced the future as it was. My father faced the future as he wished it to be.

Nineteen-thirty-three was a year to remember, a year of great changes for the country and the world, and for me in my own small world. I would begin my first year of high school (albeit still at Herman Ridder Junior High School). I was entering my freshman year as my brother started his senior year at James Monroe High School. In my brother's eyes I suddenly became someone he could talk to, at least on an academic level.

My brother was a mathematics and science scholar but barely got by in English or history, the first because he disliked writing the required essays, the latter because he had no time in his athletic schedule for the necessary history reading assignments. With very little persuasion, I was writing his essays and making outlines of the material in his history book assignments. I was so happy to be able to do something for my brother in exchange for his acceptance of me as a sister and friend.

I illustrated his science experiments and was told that his science notebook was a model for the class. My brother and I became a team.

I began to see Mac in a new light, not totally the independent, noncaring person he seemed to be. He let me know how much my help meant to him and eventually we spoke of other things than school. I discovered that my brother loved classical music and read more than just pulp fiction, especially historical novels. Suddenly we had a different picture of each other.

One day, I felt secure enough to ask him why he seemed so uninvolved in our family life. He told me that there was nothing he could do to change it for the better so he ignored it and made the best of his life. I questioned his attitude toward my father. "Pop is a real old-fashioned father. His nose is always in books or papers. He doesn't know anything about playing ball and he doesn't want to. So I go to ball games with Uncle Irving. Pop is Pop. He's closer to you because you don't need him to toss a ball or talk to him about teams. Do you understand?"

I nodded and now had another picture of relationships.

The next day I said good-bye to the neighborhood, to the school, the street, the ferry slip, the marshes, the neighbors—

and my room. I said good-bye to my street friends and the candy-store man, Louie. We said good-bye to a way of life that would end with our move to an apartment house in the city. My father said good-bye to his own home on a little plot of land which gave him his dream of being a landowner, even though he didn't really own the house.

On a chilly, gray day in March 1933, Franklin Delano Roosevelt took the oath of office as thirty-second president of the United States. In his inaugural address he asked Congress for broad powers "to wage a war against the [economic] emergency as . . . if we were invaded by a foreign foe." He used these powers to turn the country around from the Great Depression.

Also in March 1933, goose-stepping to a different drummer, Adolf Hitler was given extraordinary powers by the Reichstag. He used these powers to create a dictatorship, turning Germany and the world into an inferno.

On December 15, 1933, Utah's vote on the eighteenth amendment put the repeal effort over the top, and Prohibition came to an end. Ironically, now that it was legal to make, sell, and consume alcoholic beverages, my father no longer had the house, the basement, or the still.

In December 1933, with little money, no job, and finally no dreams, my father moved our family to an apartment near Boston Road, just one step ahead of the city marshal and eviction. We left Clason Point, and we never went back.

EPILOGUE

$\mathcal{T}$he move to the Boston Road apartment was only the first in a series of moves during those desolate years. "It's cheaper to move than pay the rent" was a phrase I heard often, as we got two months' concession on several apartments on Longfellow Avenue, Bryant Avenue, Minford Place, and East 174th Street in the Bronx.

During the first hundred days after his inauguration in 1933, Franklin Roosevelt set in motion machinery for social reform, banking reform, and labor reform needed to put America back to work, but through most of the decade of the thirties evidences of what has been called "a period of national disgrace" remained. Some men were able to find menial or odd jobs to earn a meager living. Other men traveled from city to city, from state to state, alone or with a family, hitch-

hiking or riding the rails, to find food and shelter and any kind of work to feed their families. There were still Hoovervilles around the city in vacant lots, near river banks, and in parks. My father pointed these out to me and again said, "There but for the grace of God, go I."

Over the next few years economic recovery was gradually achieved. As the country got back on its feet, so did my father. When Prohibition was repealed, he opened a distillery in New Jersey and a bottling plant on Wales Avenue in the Bronx. I had no idea how he managed to finance his business, but the money rolled in. We moved to a building with an elevator on Crotona Park East, a first step up the ladder to a family fortune.

As war clouds gathered over Europe, our country, despite isolationism, prepared for war. My brother was drafted and sent to France. My father became involved in government contracts, manufacturing paper fasteners for the duplicate and triplicate forms needed in a bureaucratic system. With money in his pocket, he set his sights on his first love, a home and land of his own. He bought a small brick bungalow in the summer rental area of Long Beach, Long Island. Before the summer of 1942 was over, we moved to a larger red-brick house—with a spacious backyard—in a year-round residential section. Between 1942 and 1946, we moved to bigger and better houses, eventually occupying an ocean-view Tudor mansion with nine bedrooms, to be used in time by friends and relatives. Every house added to the fulfillment of my father's American dream.

My mother, still a worrier, waited for the bubble to burst—and it did! In 1946, my father purchased his ultimate dream—a thirty-seven-acre, rundown chicken farm in Rhinebeck, New York. He was going to restore the farm and become a gentleman farmer, hiring a local farmer to run it. He did not own the farm—the farm owned him. He not only lost the farm, but also all the Long Beach property he mortgaged to save it.

In a last desperate attempt to salvage some of his property, he became involved in an illegal stock-market scheme. It backfired. A judge decided to make an example of an elderly, middle-class, white man and sentenced my father to one year in prison. My father spent the next eight months at Rikers Island in the prison hospital. After one visit, he asked me not to come again. He said he could not abide my loss of dignity by being searched as I landed on the island. I realized he did not want me to witness his loss of dignity—in his prison garb.

My mother's constant refrain, "Someday, Albert, the law is going to catch up with you and your shenanigans, and you're going to wind up in jail" came true.

When he was discharged, he seemed changed—extremely quiet and beaten. But my father could never admit defeat, and despite very poor health, would get involved in yet another business or scheme to find his dream at the end of the rainbow. At one time he even conducted a stationery business from a bed in Roosevelt Hospital, involving doctors and nurses as his aides.

My father was a friend to everyone. My mother lived in his shadow, enduring the seesaw life that he made for us. It was a shock to all who knew her when my mother died suddenly, just before Thanksgiving in 1952. She succumbed to a heart attack, without warning, seeming not to fight to live. I still wonder how much my father's zest for life—on his terms—contributed to her shortened life.

The father of my childhood was a miracle worker. He made life exciting; he made the impossible possible. He gave me aspirations. As I look back now, I see my father as a man with an intense desire to stay alive. To stay alive he had to have dreams; dreams bigger than life were his only means of survival.

In 1964, after undergoing extensive surgery related to his latest medical problem, diabetes, he decided to check out of Roosevelt Hospital. Knowing his prowling habits, the nurses hid his street clothes. Nevertheless, he left one evening, "borrowing" clothes much too large for his frail body. He limped out of the hospital, crawled up flights of stairs and arrived at my apartment door. I was married by then. When we saw him leaning against the door frame, I screamed, "Are you crazy? What are you doing here? How did the hospital let you out in this condition?"

As I took a deep breath, my husband continued the tirade.

"How can you walk on that?" He pointed to my father's bandaged stump. He had had his foot amputated. "Are you trying to kill yourself? Are you nuts?" My father looked at us as if we had lost our minds.

"Are you two crazy? Can I come in? Can I just sit down? Stop yelling at me!" he screamed at us. He limped to a chair, raised his foot to the ottoman, and leaned his head back against the chair. Color returned to his face.

"Now let me ask you something. Where does the Malach hamoves [the Angel of Death] look for a sick man first? In a hospital! Well, when he comes to my bed tonight, I won't be there! Let him try and find me. So, here I am."

There was no argument against his brand of logic. That was what his life was all about. Having been told as a teenager that he was not expected to live, he believed all along that he was living on borrowed time.

He survived a lifetime of life-threatening illnesses, the loss of a foot, failing eyesight, the desperate years of the Depression, and even eight months in jail, without any words of bitterness or placing blame on others. He was a survivor. It was all a part of living—and living is what he did well. Despite constant pain, he woke each dawn to meet a new day, a new challenge, and enjoyed the joke he was playing on life—staying alive no matter what the cost. My father gave me the ability to look to the future for the better things to come. From my mother I inherited the fear that even if I could achieve that dream, the bubble might eventually burst. Survival is individual. I found mine as a child in the unconditional love both my mother and father gave me.